THE CHARLIE BARBER TREATMENT

The story behind *The Charlie Barber Treatment* is, as Carole Lloyd admits, "a bit of a fairy tale really". The book was her first and was written during the six weeks of a school summer holiday when the author, a teacher by profession, had some spare time. On completion she sent the manuscript to an agent, who sent it to Julia MacRae Books, who promptly published it. The book was well reviewed on publication, shortlisted for the Whitbread Award and highly commended for the Carnegie Medal, whose selection panel praised the novel for "expressing emotion without sentimentality", for being "honest" and "humorous" and for its "excellent characterisation".

The book itself, however, despite having an element of romance, is by no means a fairy tale. The story it tells is one, initially at least, of great sorrow as fifteen-year-old Simon Walters tries to come to terms with a family tragedy. "It is not really a love story. It is more to do with how Simon copes. The basic idea behind it is that he suppresses his grief – until he meets Charlie Barber." A sequel to the book is in preparation.

A teacher since 1970, Carole Lloyd currently divides her time between writing. supervising students on teaching practi━━━━ ━━ ━━━ A Level English and D━━━━ ━━ ━━━━━ ━━━━ry, where she liv━━ ━━━━ ━━━━ ━━━ ━━━━━━ on.

D1464424

THE Charlie Barber TREATMENT

CAROLE LLOYD

WALKER BOOKS
LONDON

First published 1989 by Julia MacRae Books
This edition published 1990 by Walker Books Ltd
87 Vauxhall Walk, London SE11 5HJ

© 1989 Carole Lloyd
Cover illustration © 1989 Bill Butcher

Printed in Great Britain by
Cox and Wyman Ltd, Reading, Berkshire

British Library Cataloguing in Publication Data
Lloyd, Carole
The Charlie Barber treatment.
I. Title
823'.914 [F]
ISBN 0-7445-1488-6

Contents

Chapter
ONE

It had been a wet and windy Friday just before Easter, Simon remembered. The Crock had insisted, sadistically, that they should not allow the weather to crush their spirit and he had sent them out to play rugby in the slime that passed for a playing field. They had returned nearly an hour later like melting chocolate rabbits, cavorting and besmirching the changing rooms, leaving little muddy globules in their wake but, after a shower, Simon had felt good. He had played well. Even Crockford had noticed.

"Well done, lad," he'd said as he loped by, his thinning hair glued to his pink scalp with rain and sludge. The muscles sagged a little now, the T-shirted belly ballooned above the tracksuit's elastic and yet still he moved with the nonchalant authority of a hero. Rumour had it that he had once played for England. Simon had smiled at the compliment, in spite of trying not to, and then covered himself by acting the fool.

"Well done, lad," he mimicked and strode along behind Crockford, enjoying the giggles of his mates.

A pile of disgusting kit still had to be considered, however. He'd wondered whether to rinse off the worst as soon as he got home, to give it to his mum along with a detailed apology or simply to throw it in the washing basket as usual and hope to be out of the house when she found it. Cramming the lot into a plastic bag intended to hold only his boots, he had then become interested in a nearby conversation and the decision had never been taken.

In unrepeatable detail Kevin Halligan was describing the new girl in the fourth year who, in three short weeks at the school, had established herself in everyone's consciousness. A high-profile person if ever there was one, Simon thought, but nevertheless he laughed with everyone else and pictured with shining clarity the visions that Kevin had recently viewed and was currently describing. You could always trust in Kevin's talent as a raconteur if you didn't mind too much about the artistic blending of embroidered truth and sheer invention. Such was his clownish influence that Simon found himself agreeing, over lunch, to attend the end-of-term disco that evening as a partner for Kevin's lady's friend, only half hoping that his blind date might be slightly more refined than the siren he'd already heard so much about.

The afternoon had passed in the usual Friday haze of suppressed restlessness. The Physics lesson had been a bore with only notes to be copied from a battered textbook while a weary English teacher marked dreary essays and demanded silence, which she never got. Bulging Bessie was away for a week on a course and Science was no fun without her. Their complicated calculations regarding the volume of flesh contained, just, by the stretched threads of her hand-knitted jumpers added a competitive edge to the proceedings. Moreover, changes of underwear or sweater could wreak havoc with previous estimates, but today she was away and the game was off.

Just before the bell Shylock had shuffled in, no doubt to check that they had behaved themselves. Rasping his plump fingers together like quilted emery boards, he had asked in acid tones whether Kevin, who sat at the front and often pretended to be as thick as he looked, had made as many boobs as usual.

"No, sir. I'm keeping abreast of things now," Kevin answered innocently. Shylock hadn't even smiled but had slunk away, a little bespectacled ferret, destined to haunt the Science block forever, and Simon had smothered a sudden rush of sympathy. According to legend, Mr. Holmes had been cheerily nicknamed 'Sherlock' once upon a time but years of penny-pinching pettiness and exposure to blind ignorance had engendered a mean spirit. He dispensed no mercy and had become forever Shylock. Only Bessie could bring a twinkle to the slaty eyes as she squeezed herself into the prep room where he lurked in quivering expectation. Simon had once seen her wink at the lab technician as she jammed the little man against a filing cabinet. She was a good sort. He imagined her sculpted from foam rubber, Botticelli style, dead comfy and, when she explained things, he understood. One day she'd make a lovely granny.

The last lesson was worse. He'd opted for History, after much consideration, because it seemed important to know how generations of people had lived and dealt with their situations, but destiny had decreed that he should be placed in the wrong group. Dr. Lealman could not control a class, especially not a disenchanted fourth year, and the last lesson on a Friday must have been for him like the hell at the end of a long, dark mineshaft of a week. Sometimes he went looking for a missing book and didn't come back. Sometimes he battled bravely to the end, not seeing the missiles, not hearing the jibes, not looking any of them in the eyes. It was a kind of crude entertainment that should have become boring long ago but never had. They were all to blame, he and them, for wasted time, a wasted subject and wasted minds. Yet the man was an expert, a dedicated historian who had written books. He was a dapper little man, always neat and precise, with a bland, open stare. His weakness in the face of loutish boys and malicious, insolent girls was uncomfortable to watch. Simon frequently wanted to hit him.

Fortunately the lesson was curtailed for a scrappy Easter assembly at the end of the day. Some sports colours were given out to the lucky few, there were the usual boring announcements about recent and coming events and they finished up with "There is a green hill. . .", surely the most turgid hymn tune ever written. Simon stood awkwardly in the crooked line, waiting for it all to end. He remembered how he'd enjoyed the singing at junior school, priding himself on knowing the words and not feeling in the least self-conscious. When he came here he'd sung at first, just as enthusiastically. They all had until they realised how thin the sound seemed in the high-roofed hall. In the second year he'd sung very quietly. In the third year he'd mimed, like a goldfish, or fitted normal conversation to the lines. Now it was the fashion to refuse to take part at all or to sing off-key very loudly, so he'd stood mute and waited for the last notes to signify that the term was finally over.

It was strange but he could even remember the bus journey home that day. The coach was always packed, seventy children on a fifty-two seater, but wet days meant macs, umbrellas, damp clothing and a pungent body steam mixing with the clouds from the back-seat smokers. Simon dashed for a seat midway down, equidistant from the rabble at the back and from Barry Andrews at the front who was invariably green by the time he reached his village and sometimes sick beforehand. As one of the three 'bus prefects' Simon had quickly discovered, like George, the driver, that a fast journey and a low profile were the best combination. Outnumbered in a confined space they had learnt to avoid confrontation at all costs so, when Sarah and Karen shrieked like banshees or Dave Wakefield launched forth with his limited Anglo-Saxon vocabulary or the smell of singed upholstery wafted down the gangway, Simon tightened his lips and looked downwards while George slid the great bus into gear and concentrated on the road.

Two girls flopped into the single seat next to Simon. The one in the middle was Susan, a precocious and bubbling second-year with a passion for himself, no less. To be adored, even by a child, is not wholly unpleasant. Consequently he had found himself smiling in response when she called down corridors, across the dining room, or into the common room, "Hi, Simon". Now here she was again, thigh to thigh with him, being willingly pushed by her giggling friend on the end. He assumed his look of superior, wry amusement as she blushed, then he turned away to watch the raindrops being diverted across the window as the coach gathered speed. Susan wouldn't thank him for witnessing her embarrassment and he didn't want to cloud her judgement of him. He had felt powerful at that moment, a puppet-master. He had turned back, smiling.

"Have you got enough room, Sue?"

"Oh yes. Thanks. We're OK."

He wondered what she'd do if he fulfilled her fantasies, if he grabbed her here and now and publicly took advantage. She was quite promising really, already filling out nicely and her teeth were white and even when she smiled, so the rest of the journey had passed pleasurably as he toyed with an imaginary Susan while the real thing sat ecstatic but ignored at his side.

By the time he reached his stop the coach was three-quarters-empty though he still had to squeeze past Susan and friend. Kevin followed him down the steps and then called back to George.

"Thank you, my good man." George grinned and closed the doors, pulling away suddenly and almost sandwiching a battered Fiesta which had been rash enough to try to overtake him.

"Damn, he almost minced the Deputy Head then, Si."

"Typical incompetence of the British working man, Kev."

"See ya tonight, mate."

"Yeah, OK."

They had gone their separate ways in confident expectation of meeting again very soon. Simon glanced up as he slung the heavy bag over his shoulder in exactly the way one was told not to do in crowded corridors. Susan was waving frantically from the back window of the receding bus so he nodded in casual acknowledgement and switched to a contemplation of his plans. No homework tonight at least – a languid bath, a choice of smells to splash all over and the prospect of a good time.

By the time he got home he was wet through. He wouldn't be seen dead in a mac, although some of the fifth year had taken to navy coats and rolled umbrellas, parodying the business men they hoped to become. Kev would end up like that – fast cars, fast women and no conscience. Kev would breeze into the disco tonight, outrageous to look at and fast-talking, half-admired and half-repellent, not caring what people thought. That's why they were friends, thought Simon, because they were opposites. Simon envied Kevin's easy banter and his independence. Kevin picked Simon's brains. He always dismissed serious observations with a joke but you knew that he listened because he quoted things back at you weeks later, when it suited him.

There were three bottles of milk by the back door and as he bent to pick them up his bag fell forward and hit him across the right ear. He straightened angrily, threw his bag to the ground and swore. Then, lifting the three slippery, cold bottles carefully he was forced to clutch them to his chest as he used his other hand to turn the door knob and his shoulder to nudge the door, which resisted firmly. One bottle slithered from his grasp and smashed on the concrete, showering the step, the door, the path, his shoes and trousers with gold-top full cream. The two watery skimmed milks remained intact in the crook of his arm. With an effort of will he controlled the hands that carefully replaced the bottles on the ground before trying the back door again. It was definitely locked and there was neither sound nor smell emanating from the house. Often, on cold or wet days, there'd be tea and toast waiting for him and hot water for a bath. His mum didn't usually work on Fridays. He enjoyed coming home to a welcome. Now he trudged round to the front, annoyed with her.

With cold, numb fingers, hastily wiped on the stiff wet

cloth of his trousers, he groped for a front door key in his inside pocket. A few coins, a packet of Polos and a comb – but no key. Then he remembered. A few nights ago he'd left it in the door as he hurried in. His dad had found it next morning and had yelled up the stairs at him, calling him stupid and infantile for leaving a key in the front door all night.

"We could have all been burgled or murdered in our beds."

"But you'd bolted the door inside like you always do so no one could just walk in."

"Someone could have stolen the key and used it later."

"Yes, but no one did so it's alright – anyway sorry, Dad."

Simon had learnt that to apologise early, even if you weren't that sorry, was a good tactic. It took the wind out of people's sails.

"Well, just be more careful in future. Think."

All his life Simon had been exhorted to think. When he'd knocked over his Ribena or spilt ink or smashed a rose bush with a football it had always been, "For goodness' sake, Simon, think what you're doing." And he'd thought, I'm clumsy and awkward and accidents come looking for me, and thinking seemed to make it worse. When he thought about not spilling drinks, when he tried to be careful, even when he tried to be helpful, things went wrong. He could have left the milk outside but in trying to bring it in he'd smashed it. The skimmed milk was for Mum and Dad. The gold-top was his, for cornflakes or sugar puffs, and now it had soaked into his socks. Sod's law! And the key that would let him in to a warm house, a hot bath and dry clothes was, he knew, lying on the hall table where he'd left it. He'd seen it that morning, meant to pick it up and then forgotten about it. He peered through the letter-box to check. He could see it clearly, lying on top of a white envelope which contained a cheque for the Ski Trip which should have been paid in by today to secure a place on next February's expedition to Austria. It never rains but it pours – and Simon had lifted his face to the heavens and let it rain to its heart's content into his eyes, into his mouth and down his neck. Surrender to it, he thought. *C'est la vie!*

He was nothing if not philosophical. He'd been taught the hard way, in primary school, that life can be unfair. You get bullied or ignored or laughed at and if you show you care they do it some more. "It's a tough world," his mum had said. "I can't help you, Simon. Get in there and cope. They'll soon pick on someone else," and eventually they had, though not before he'd suffered more than enough. Now he wasn't a victim any more. He was cool and self-contained and learning, from people like Kev, that the sky wouldn't fall down if you did your own thing. So now, thoroughly saturated, he made a quick decision. Mum was obviously out. There was no radio playing, no cooking smell. He could either sit here indefinitely or break in. The bathroom window might be open.

Round at the back of the house he surveyed the situation. The bathroom top light was slightly ajar and by balancing on the framework of the conservatory that ran the full length of the back of the house he could reach it, open the large window and get in. He looked guiltily around at the empty gardens, as if he were really intent on burglary and it was not his own house he was entering. There was no one else out in the storm, no nosy neighbour likely to challenge him or, worse still, to phone the police.

Heart pounding, with a mixture of daring and fear of falling, he had mountaineered his way in, using fingertips and toe-holds, balancing his weight, testing the brickwork. From dustbin to window-ledge to garage roof to conservatory he'd manoeuvred. The worst moment had been when he was travelling sideways from metal strut to metal strut, face to the house wall, feeling his way along and hearing the glass panes creak under his weight. One slip and he'd be through the glass and ripped to pieces. It had been a ludicrous idea and he should have thought it through. He had stood still a moment, fighting back the panic, realising that he had no choice but to go on. Moments later he was inside, mission accomplished, and exhilarated. He felt happier seeing his own dressing-gown on the hook and his own soap-on-a-rope, misshapen and squidgy, dangling from a tap. He realised then that he'd opened the window quietly, slithered in as silently as he could and clenched his teeth instead of yelling when he'd banged his shin on the taps; he'd behaved for all the world like a real intruder. Now he felt foolish.

"Mum?" His shout seemed to bounce back from the walls. "Mum – it's Jack the Ripper, come to get yer..." She was definitely not in. With relish he began to strip off the wet things and left them in a sodden heap on the bathroom floor. The shoes and socks he threw into the bath. The milk was slimy and would smell unless he soaked it all away. He turned on the taps, added some bubble bath and then threw in the trousers too. He'd bath himself later. A brisk rub-down with a warm towel, tracksuit on and then to make a drink, a sandwich and retrieve his bag from by the back door. The smashed bottle he'd deal with when the rain stopped. He'd coped rather well.

Purposefully he moved from room to room, bringing the house to life – electric fire on in the living room, record onto the hi-fi, kettle on for coffee and something to eat. There was a plastic bag full of shopping on the kitchen table, next to his mother's handbag. That was lucky. She usually bought goodies at the weekends. It didn't take long to find a pack of Mars bars. He made coffee and was half-way through the Mars bar when he remembered the bath. The bubbles were impressive but the water still an inch below the rim. Again he had a sense of a lucky break, though the thought of his leather shoes at the bottom was not very cheering. He'd only intended to run an inch or two of water. Still, they'd have all weekend to dry out. His mum would moan but he'd live with that.

Where was she? She'd been shopping, her bag was in the kitchen, so she couldn't be at work. If she'd popped round to a neighbour she would have been back before he got home from school, and have realised he hadn't got a key when she saw it on the table. He tried to think back to breakfast. Had she said anything about going anywhere?

She hadn't had any breakfast. She'd been in bed and Dad had said she wasn't well. She had been having headaches recently and had got one this morning. Yet she had been up and been shopping. Perhaps she was having a lie-down, or was even fast asleep. Suddenly uneasy about his behaviour – the breaking in, the shoes in the bath and the pounding of the music – he hurried to her bedroom and then on second thoughts dashed downstairs to switch off the music before investigating. He had, he remembered, paused and listened before opening the door gently.

She was not where he'd expected to see her, curled up in the duvet. He was about to leave the room when he saw her feet or, more accurately, a foot on the floor at the far side of the bed.

She was lying, still with her anorak on, face-down on the carpet, just as if she had slid sideways off the bed and gone to sleep on the rug instead. She'd obviously fainted. What do you do when people have fainted? Give them air? Open collars? He couldn't think. He knelt down and shook her gently. "Mum, Mum. Wake up. I'm home. Come on, it's alright now. Mum?" Air – she needed air. He opened a window and the wind and the rain swept in. She'd soon stir now.

"Mum, come on, let's get you into bed." He turned her over. Her eyes were closed and her face looked smooth. There was neither the frown that creased her forehead when she was angry or unwell, nor the dimples that came when she laughed. She looked calm and smooth and very cold. Simon hadn't the slightest doubt. He stood up and closed the window to shut out the noise and the damp and then he pulled the duvet off the bed and snuggled it around her. She looked more decent that way. It seemed unnatural to sprawl on the floor, with your outdoor clothes still on, at her age.

Who to ring? That was a problem. Do you ring the doctor or the hospital? The undertaker? Not yet surely?

He'd have to phone his dad to ask, to tell him about... At the bottom of the stairs his legs gave way; he felt very sick and very faint. He sat with his head down, listening to the thumping in his chest and the surging in his veins. It seemed ages before he could think straight.

"For goodness' sake, Simon, think!"

It was at least 5.20 p.m. He'd noticed the time when he'd gone to switch off the hi-fi. His father would probably have left his office to catch the train. Even if he phoned and just caught him, Dad wouldn't be able to get home any quicker. Best to tell him when he got home. Suzie was at college, too far away to help him now. What could he say to them? How would he tell them? Perhaps he'd better double-check. Perhaps he'd been mistaken. Perhaps she had moved by now.

He couldn't remember walking back upstairs; only that moment, when he knew from the pallor of that calm mask that she hadn't moved a millimetre, stayed with him. He'd come down, found the doctor's number, asked him to call and then sat and waited on the stairs. He'd let the doctor in and the doctor had gone up and come down and then said he was sorry and how could he get hold of his father. When his father arrived, Mrs. Green from next door had met him in the drive and burst into tears. The doctor had waylaid him in the hall and had broken the news Simon had not known how to convey. Dad had appeared in the doorway like a stranger, somehow shrivelled, his grey face distorted, but the voice was familiar.

"Simon. What happened?"

Simon opened his mouth and no words came. He shook his head. He didn't know what had happened. They'd never know what had happened. He felt as if he were choking. His head was bursting, his chest burning. He wanted to yell, to explode, but no sound came.

"Simon found her, Mr. Walters. It's been a great ordeal for him. He's been very sensible. He called me right away." His father melted into an armchair but kept one hand on each arm, as if he were afraid of slipping further.

"She'd been dead some hours, Mr. Walters. There was nothing we could do."

Simon watched his father wither a little more and felt only anger. Was it only this morning he'd breezed in and announced, "You're on your own this morning, mate. Mum's got a headache so it's fend-for-yourself-day today. These women!" He'd gone off to work and left her to die on her own. Simon had taken his time getting up and nearly missed the bus. He'd raced out of the house, forgetting the key and the ski money, yelling, "Bye," as he left but not checking, not seeing if she needed anything. He hadn't understood that she was ill. Dad should have realised. He slept with her, for God's sake! He should have realised and explained, made sure that Simon understood. Now it was too late, would always be too late. He looked up to see his father sitting silently, his face frozen. The doctor's hand was on his father's shoulder. Mrs. Green appeared with a tray of tea and the doctor smiled in approval. Simon looked at the three of them – perfect casting all round: the shabby uncertain housewife, the smooth professional in his tailored suit and the shattered husband, still in his overcoat, sagging like a battered teddy bear. Strange how crises happened with your coat on in this family. Simon suddenly saw himself, ungainly and unmanly, naked under the torn old tracksuit, barefooted and pathetic. It was his own fault. He'd been too strong, too controlled when the moment came. He should have slipped and gone through the glass roof after all, as he was meant to. He'd defied death, faced danger and escaped from it, only to find that death had already outwitted him. It comes when you least expect it, not when you're alert. Life is funny when you stop to think about it. It never rains but it pours. You have to laugh.

He'd still been giggling spasmodically when they'd tucked him up in bed. He remembered the doctor saying, "He'll be alright for a few hours. I've given him a shot."

Funny, thought Simon, I didn't hear a thing. And for hours he didn't.

Chapter
TWO

When the alarm rang, on the day of the funeral, Simon covered his head with his pillows and let it ring. Before long Suzie or Dad would come dashing in. They'd developed a habit of checking up on him at intervals so there was really no need to wriggle out of the warm patch to reach the off-button. This time it was Suzie.

"Are you alright, Simon?" she said, slamming a hand down on the clock. The raucous trilling stopped. It was a good invention, as harsh and insistent as it had to be, perfectly engineered for its purpose, like a siren or a screw. Or a coffin. No – not a coffin. That was camouflage for sensitive minds. Like a zip-up plastic bag. Very functional.

"Aren't you going to get up?"

He remained motionless under the covers until he heard her move away. She left his door ajar. He hated that. He liked his door closed.

Out on the landing he heard them whispering. His father sounded tired.

"Is he getting up?"

"I don't know. He wouldn't answer."

"Perhaps he's still asleep."

"Not through that racket he isn't."

"Leave him. We've got a couple of hours yet."

He heard them move in opposite directions, his dad into the bathroom and his sister down the stairs.

How can you say you've got a couple of hours? A couple of hours before what? Before they fill in the hole? Before the mass invasion of po-faced relatives? Before he needed to get up? He emerged to look at the time. Eight-thirty. He'd got until about ten. After that they really wouldn't allow him to fester behind closed doors any longer. He tip-toed out of bed and closed his door properly, very quietly so they wouldn't know he was up.

By lunch-time it will all be over, he thought to himself. They'd be back in this house, the three of them, with nothing hanging over their heads but time. Suzie and Mrs. Green had made sandwiches and little cakes and malt-bread slices. They'd borrowed extra china cups and saucers from friends down the road. Simon had mechanically dusted, and vacuumed the carpets. He'd refused to clean the toilets.

"You'll have to do it sometime, Simon."

In the end Suzie and Dad had cleaned the bathroom while Simon tidied the front garden and manicured the lawn. "For the flowers," Dad had said.

The house was immaculate. For Mum's sake, they'd explained. For the visitors. Suzie had worked long hours, cleaning, cooking, shopping, sorting, never still. She had come home the next day, not having got the message, about phoning, until the morning. When she arrived it was all over. She had wandered around, dazed and disbelieving, for hours and then hounded Simon for information, becoming irritable when he didn't say what she wanted to hear. He'd offered up trivial details.

"What was she like, when you found her?"

"I've already told you."

"I need to know. Describe it exactly."

"She had her blue jacket on, and there was fluff under the bed, and Dad's slippers."

About four o'clock in the afternoon Kevin had phoned

and Simon had answered.

"Where were you last night? I phoned you but it was engaged all the time. I thought you were coming?"

"Sorry. I couldn't," said Simon.

"Is that it? Sorry I couldn't? What was I supposed to do with two women?"

"Sounds like your idea of a good time, mate."

"Yeah, well. It worked out quite well as it happened. You missed a cracker, my boy." Simon didn't answer. It all seemed so irrelevant. "Anyway. What were you up to?"

"Had to stay in. Family...you know."

"Daddy put you in detention then?" Kevin's mocking tone gave him the cue.

"No," he said cruelly. "My Mum's died." There was silence at the other end. "See you around, ок?"

"Sure," Kevin said. Simon could feel his discomfort and did nothing to help. This is how it would be.

"Bye," he said and replaced the receiver gently.

Suzie was standing, furious, on the stairs.

"How could you?" She almost spat at him.

"What?"

"Just say it like that, as if...as if..." She meant as if it wasn't important.

"What was I s'posed to say? She'd kicked the bucket? Snuffed it?"

"Don't!"

He'd left her there, half-way up and half-way down, and walked away. There aren't any words, not really, he'd thought. People who believed in God had words but, in the end, it all came down to this. "My mother's died," he repeated to himself. It was the word 'dead' he wouldn't use.

They had over a week of dreamlike abnormality punctuated by little dramas. The first few days saw a steady stream of uncomfortable visitors, offering sympathy and help, never defining anything they were actually prepared to do. Even Nora Turner, a loud, bulbous woman from across the road, whom Simon remembered only as the old bat who'd stopped them playing on her grass verge when they were children, arrived. He opened the door to her.

"Simon, pet. I've just heard. Is your dad in?"

He let her in and Dad's welcome was surprisingly genuine. Even his sister, who'd shouted many a rude remark at Nora in her youth, sat in on the interview. He went off to make yet another pot of tea, following a kind of measured routine, investing the task with a sense of the ritual it had become. He knew what they'd be saying and couldn't bear to hear it any more, all these semi-strangers picking over the tit-bits of information, feeding. His family were the talk of the village. At first Simon hadn't gone out at all. Those who had called early had become important. He imagined them, in the shop, in the bus queue, criss-crossing in the road. "Pass it on. Pass it on." He'd seen them over fences, at front doors, in the gardens, shaking heads and nodding towards their house. "Well I never! Who would have thought it?"

Usually, when he got back to the lounge with the tea, they'd reached the "Of course, it was Simon who found her" stage. He'd perfected the weak smile that dared them to probe further. A few did.

"Oh my dear! Whatever did you do?"

After the first few non-committal shrugs Dad had taken to answering for him. When he got back this time batty Nora was in full flow.

"Well, like I said to our Ivy, there's no accounting for it. *He* knows best, I always say. Course, our George – that's my Tom's youngest brother – hasn't ever been the same, not since, and we keep an eye on him when we can. Always see him at Christmas, unless the weather's bad." Simon was bewildered. He glanced enquiringly at Suzie who frowned back. Dad had a glazed expression but Nora didn't seem to notice. "Mind you, our Annie did say, just before, she felt a bit tired but then you do, don't you? Nobody thought it was anything serious. Did *she* say anything?" The question, suddenly dropped in, took his father by surprise.

"No," said Simon.

"It's always worse like that, when it's sudden. It's the shock, you see. When you're not expecting it."

What's she telling us this for? thought Simon. Over the cup of tea she told them more about Annie, who'd dropped dead of a stroke, and Mr. Evans along the road, who'd collapsed while pulling his rhubarb. Mrs. Evans had called the police when he'd been missing most of the day. They'd done half the woods and the duck pond before a police dog sniffed him out in the garden. "It was very tall rhubarb, you see."

Simon took the tray out to make sure she wasn't offered another cup. When she finally left she remembered why she'd come. She turned her papery, moon-like face on them and said, "If there's anything I can do..."

"No," said Simon. "Not a sodding thing!" Dad had been livid with him. "But they're vultures, Dad. She doesn't care. They're just nosy."

"Some, maybe, but people try their best."

"Why do you tell them? Why d'you tell them everything?"

"You can at least be civil."

"Not to her. Not to people like her."

"Then keep out of it. As long as you're in this house you don't insult grown-ups." Grown-ups! He'd handled this better than any of them. "It's disrespectful. People were fond of your mother." It was always 'your mother'. Dad hadn't said her name or 'my wife' since it happened.

Suzie seemed to understand. "You don't need to sit through it all if you don't want to. You can stay out of the way when they come." So he had.

He wasn't going to be able to stay out of the way today. They were all going to be on show, centre-stage. He pulled on jeans and an ancient T-shirt. The suit they'd made him buy could hang in the wardrobe until the last moment. Barefooted he went downstairs, on legs that didn't quite belong, and helped himself to Dad's muesli and milk. The first spoonful went round and round in his mouth. I've got to swallow it by ten o'clock, he thought. Still chewing, he poured the rest down the sink, running the tap and forcing the lumps down the holes with his spoon.

"There's tea in the pot," Suzie said. She was polishing teaspoons with a tea-towel. He took one of the shiny ones and used it to load coffee granules into a mug. "The kettle's just boiled," she added. He switched it on again. "Would you like some toast?" He shook his head and concentrated on the kettle. The spout was furred up with lime. It seemed to take ages to come back to the boil. In the end he couldn't wait and filled the mug with water only seconds away from boiling point. He took it back to his room and propped himself up on the bed with pillows and cushions. He felt like cotton wool, weightless.

He hadn't expected to feel so scared. It was, after all, merely a ceremony, the ritualised signing and sealing, the rubber stamp. The worst moment had been last Wednesday, when the doctor had called to explain that the post mortem was complete and 'arrangements could now be made'.

"Just as I expected, Mr. Walters. Quite straightforward. A massive haemorrhage to the brain. Very sudden, very quick. I doubt she knew much about it."

"Haemorrhage?" Simon had said. "There wasn't any blood."

"No. It's internal bleeding, Simon. As I said, she wouldn't have known much about it." He could see that the doctor was kind, concerned for them all. "Let me know if there is anything I can do," he'd called as he scurried away to his next patient.

In the end he hadn't needed to go with Dad to the undertakers. Mr. R. F. Unwin, Funeral Director, had come to them and impressed Simon with his calm, business-like approach, asking questions about cars and flowers, for all the world as if they were organising a wedding. He does this every day of his life, thought Simon. We must be one of the easy ones. They'd sat, all three of them, agreeing on coffin wood, handles, floral tributes and hymns. No one shed a tear. What did they want in the paper? If he phoned it through straightaway they might just get it in tomorrow's edition of the weekly newspaper. They'd agreed to keep it simple. When he'd gone they all sat silently thinking their own thoughts. Eventually, as Suzie's eyes brimmed with tears, she got up.

"I'd better do some shopping," she said. "Anyone want to come?"

Dad had forced himself. "I'll run you up to the shop, save carrying it." They'd left him alone in the house with his visions. He had deliberately punished himself – Mum in the hands of strangers, men with white coats and scalpels, a body slapped down on a slab, like a fish, incisions and blood... His eyes had burned but he had not cried. He'd hugged himself in the armchair, facing the facts, imagining the worst that he could imagine. Nothing could hurt her any more, least of all today. Today was disposal day for 'the remains'. He was glad of the system. He wouldn't have to see what 'remained'. He simply had to get through it, with dignity. He would put himself on automatic pilot like he did when he went to the dentist or went in to an exam. "It'll be over before you know it," she'd always said to him. Ironic when you came to think of it. He drank half the coffee and then sank with his eyes closed, dozing.

A ring at the door woke him. It was twenty to ten. He climbed ponderously off the bed and drew back the curtains. There were three wreaths and a bunch of flowers in line along the edge of the lawn. His stomach turned over. He'd known they would come. Tears pricked. I will not cry, he told himself. I will not cry for them all to see. A man was walking across the grass carrying another bouquet and wearing a wreath over each arm, like jugglers' hoops. He laid them at regular intervals and adjusted the little tickets that nestled in the leaves. Simon had a sudden urge to know who'd sent them. It's not enough, he thought. There need to be lots and lots.

He shot down the stairs and out into the garden. There

were strange messages on the tiny cards. 'God bless Auntie May and Uncle Harold'. Why? What had they done? 'Rest in Peace. Mary and Reg Cooper'. Who the hell were they? People with very original minds obviously! 'With love, Mum and Gran'. That was better. He wondered if his great-grandmother would be coming. She was very old. Her skin hung in soft folds below bright, curranty eyes but because her white hair was pulled up tight into a skimpy bun, her forehead was smoother, lined but not floppy. She looked like she was melting gently in her wheelchair when they sat her in the sunshine. She always unnerved him because her eyes followed his every move when he was near her. "Old people watch children," Mum had said. "She doesn't mean any harm." The other four wreaths were from neighbours or friends. There must be a lot still to come.

"Simon. Are you going to get ready?"

"Yeah, OK."

Suzie was fussing, checking. As he came back in he heard his father in the kitchen.

"Has he done anything to help at all?"

"Leave him, Dad. Give him time."

He hurried upstairs, guilty and grateful. Step by step, slowly and automatically, he transformed himself. He'd never had a suit before. He didn't look like himself. He was ready.

As he came down the doorbell rang again. Another florist. "Over there," he said and followed the young woman who'd held out a wreath to him. She was a local girl who worked in a flower shop in Newbury, seven miles away. She smiled shyly.

"There's more in the van," she said.

"I'll help." Together they unloaded six more. The lawn was beginning to look respectable.

"Such a shame," she said. "They're so lovely but they don't last long." It could hardly be more appropriate, he thought, but he smiled back.

"They serve a purpose."

"Yes, of course," she said and, remembering their purpose, she hurried off muttering something about other calls.

"Thank you," he called.

He began to check the cards against the list in his head, calculating numbers still to come, noting the omissions. For the next half-hour he employed himself on flower duty or gate duty, receiving all callers with a polite expression, feeling adult in his dark, smart outfit. His father came out, nodded with satisfaction to see him usefully employed at last, and then followed the latest arrivals back in. He saw a glass of sherry in his father's hand. No one thought to offer him one.

Mum's Auntie Beryl from Birmingham arrived in a huge fur coat, red and flustered, travel-stained.

"This is never our Simon," she said. "Nobody told me 'e was that good-looking."

"Hello," he said. "The others are inside."

"Oooh, I can't go in yet, duck. Where's the lav? I'm bursting for a wee."

"Top of the stairs, turn left," he said.

Mum's cousin Keith followed behind, dangling his car keys.

"Good journey?" Simon asked.

"Bloody awful," he said, "but this place isn't bad is it? I could live in a place like this." You could die in a place like this too, Simon thought.

"There's sherry in the house."

"Just the job," said Keith.

Simon hadn't intended still to be out there so when the hearse slid quietly into view it took him by surprise. He'd dreaded this. All morning, while the butterflies danced in his chest, he'd been telling himself, "I'll be alright once it starts. I'll be alright once I've seen the hearse." He stood resolutely by the gate, fixing it in his mind. The coffin was pale and shining, somehow feminine, just what she would have chosen. He was surprised how small it was, almost child-size. On the top was a cross made of red roses, the one they'd ordered. He was going to be alright.

More black cars drew up, huge and purring, respectful. Men in dark coats headed towards him.

"Can we get the flowers, son?" They began to load them in, expertly, building a great hill behind the glass. Mr. Unwin recognised him and shook his hand, man to man.

"Alright, sir?"

"Fine," said Simon.

"Right, let's round them up."

And somehow he got through it. He didn't get up and yell, "Balls!" when the vicar chuntered on about God's will and eternal life. He didn't cry at all. He swallowed very hard for a minute or two as they lowered her down, the raw earth screened by green cloths of shimmery artificial grass, but he didn't cry. Suzie did. Nobody took much notice. Dad stood stony-faced. Simon knew how hard he was trying and moved closer, letting the back of his hand brush against his dad's. Dad grabbed it and held on and that was almost his undoing so Simon squeezed it and pulled free. But the rest had been easier.

Back at home he remained on his best behaviour, handing out teas and plates of food, a sidekick for his sister who had dried her eyes and taken charge. Auntie Beryl was magic. Some old lady was reminiscing in the corner, gazing with rheumy eyes at anyone who stopped to listen, like the angel of death under a black felt hat. Simon caught odd phrases, "on her mother's side, once-removed", "never should have married him", and then, loudly, "Where's the cake?" Simon took a plate of cakes over to her. She took her time, fingered five with yellow, claw-like fingers, moved them around a bit and then took the two biggest ones.

"Be quiet, our Edie, and eat your cake," said Beryl, now resplendent in a lilac frock and a string of plastic pearls. "I want to talk to our Sally's boy." He'd intended to go back after his rounds with the cake plate but there were cups to wash and teapots to fill. He never got there.

Once one person started to leave everyone began to stir fairly rapidly. Dad, Suzie and Simon stood in the hall, shaking hands and nodding like chickens. People clutched his hand in both of theirs, in lieu of words, or clapped him on both shoulders as if he'd won something. Soon only the close family were left. Simon headed for the kitchen. His grandmother was at the sink, systematically washing while Mum's sister, Janey, dried. He heard Grandma say, "Didn't our Simon look grown-up? He's done a real man's job today."

Suzie was tipping curled sandwiches into the bin. She saw him first. "Yes," she said. "Thanks, Si. You've been great."

Suzie looked at him with his mother's eyes and his mother's face. He saw how she must have been as a young girl. Grandma and Janey were looking at him too, smiling benignly. He couldn't bear it.

"What did you expect?" he said, and fled.

Chapter
THREE

The white envelope had re-appeared on the hall table during the last day of the Easter holiday.

"Don't forget your ski money," Suzie had reminded him.

"It's much too late now," he said, but his father was encouraging.

"I'm sure they'll make allowances," he argued.

"No they won't. Why should they? Anyway I don't want to go."

"Why not?"

"Because it's expensive and just before my exams and it was a daft idea in the first place." His father was amazed, understandably.

"But you spent hours convincing us that it was reasonably priced, it wouldn't affect your school work and you'd always wanted to have a go at skiing."

"I did then," Simon paused, unable to furnish a clear explanation, "now I don't." He'd seen his dad look at Suzie and Suzie had shrugged, equally bewildered. He was absolutely certain that he didn't want to go. They hadn't succeeded in persuading him and on the first day of term he'd picked up his key and deliberately left the envelope on the table. He never saw it again.

Going back to school would, he knew, be an ordeal, but

at least he hadn't been absent; everyone else would be going back after a two-week break, too, gossiping about what they'd done in the holiday, and if Kevin had done his stuff they might not ask him questions. Simon felt guilty about Kevin but he'd try to make it up to him later. On the day following the funeral Kevin had turned up on the doorstep at about ten in the morning. It must have been hard for him but he'd arrived all the same, neither clowning nor solemn, simply concerned. Simon had still been in bed and Suzie had sent Kevin up to him. He'd plonked himself on the edge of the bed, punched the curled heap playfully and begun.

"C'mon mate, wake up. I'm not staying long." Simon had dragged himself upright, sleepily, and apprehensively. "You OK?"

"Yeah. Course," he said.

"We came yesterday, me and a few of the lads, with Sandy, Jackie and that lot."

"Yes I know." Simon had seen them, out of the corner of his eye, in the pews across the back of the church, but he hadn't dared to look straight at them. "Thanks," he said.

"Couldn't do much but we just wanted you to know we were there." Simon nodded. "Would it help," Kevin went on tentatively, "if you told me about it?"

"Why?" snapped Simon. Why did people think he wanted to talk about it all the time? It was hardly likely to change anything. Kevin looked embarrassed.

"Well, you know what people are like. They all want to know, keep asking questions. If I tell them they won't need to ask you. Just thought it might help, that's all." Simon could see the logic in that.

"What do you want to know?"

"Dunno really." It was the first time Kevin had been lost for words. There was an uncomfortable silence. "You don't have to, if you don't want to," he said eventually. "I'll go, shall I? You can always phone, if you feel like it."

"No, stay," Simon said quickly. So Kevin had stayed a while. Suzie had brought them coffee and stayed to listen when she found Simon in the middle of an explanation. She'd heard it all already. He didn't tell Kevin any more than he'd told everyone else but the three of them sat and shared the story and planned the next move.

"Are you coming back to school next Monday?" Kevin asked.

"Yeah. Course I am."

"You won't need to worry about the staff, anyway. There'll be a notice up in the staff room to tell them all and they'll be told to be understanding in the circumstances."

"How do you know?"

"That old biddy next door to us has a sister who is a cleaner up there. When my dad left, Mum told the Head in case...I don't know, in case I went peculiar or something. They put up a notice and the cleaners all read it. My mum was furious and she went to see him. But that's what they do anyway."

"Yes. That's right," said Suzie. "When I was there one girl cried all day because her dog had been run over and she wouldn't tell us what was wrong but all the teachers seemed to know. In the end we asked Mrs. Crowe, our form teacher, and she told us. The girl's mother had phoned that morning and all the staff had been warned. It was Mandy Fisher, from the farm. Do you remember?"

"Yeah," said Simon. "And her dad bought her a new puppy, just like that one on the toilet paper commercial, and we both wanted one. We nearly persuaded Mum but Dad wouldn't let us."

"Mum liked animals," said Suzie. "I wish we'd had a dog or something."

"I liked your mum," Kevin suddenly announced. There was another silence until eventually he felt compelled to break it. "Anyway, I'm off now. Phone me if you feel like it. If not, I'll see you on Monday. I'll try to keep the kids off your back. See ya!" and he was gone.

"Come on." Suzie yanked the duvet. "There's work to be done."

"Sod off," he said, but he had got up all the same and

done his best to be reasonably helpful. The thought of the new term had reminded him that his sister would be going, too, leaving him to cope without her determined house-keeping. She'd been unbelievable, ministering to them both more efficiently than Mum ever had, even sorting and repairing his clothes. With Grandma and Janey she'd disposed of most of his mother's things, though he'd noticed she was wearing the engagement ring on her right hand. Dad had the wedding ring somewhere. Soon she'd be gone, back to college and a different life. It'll be easier for her, he thought, and she had gone on that Monday while he was out, during that first day at school, leaving the house redundant like an empty stage set, insubstantial.

He had felt like an actor checking his lines as he trudged towards the bus-stop. He hadn't been up this early for ages and the air smelt clean, unused. There wasn't a breath of wind. Every leaf, every twig, looked painted against a pale grey sky. It must have rained in the night for the gutters were damp and the hedges glistened under a weak sun. "All I have to do," he told himself, "is to concentrate on the work, and if people pry I'll pretend I haven't heard them." Mum had taught him, when he was very young, the Fire Escape game. If you imagined the very worst that could happen and worked out a contingency plan, then whatever happened you could deal with it. What was the very worst that could happen? He wanted neither teasing nor sympathy. Sympathy would be the worst. He'd have to show he didn't need it, like Martin what's-his-name in the third year.

This boy had been injured in a car accident and been away so long people had forgotten about him. Then he suddenly reappeared on crutches and eventually walked without them, using only a stick which served a number of purposes, for Martin and his friends. It could be used to hook girls' skirts, to poke people from two metres away, to trip first-years or even to help Martin as he struggled up flights of stairs. And all the time he went on smiling and joking and having a go at anything he could manage. Simon had seen him throwing the javelin and discus from a stand-still. He once saw him fall in a crowded corridor and yell "Timber!" as loudly as he could to warn the stampeding hordes. People had picked him up, dusted him down, given him back the stick and set him on his way but he'd refused to move until they'd given him his own bag to carry too. What a great kid! Simon had thought, and he hadn't known then what he later discovered, that the injured leg was in fact an artificial one. Some people seemed to bounce back no matter what life did to them.

Simon saw himself in the same context as he made his way down the hill. Like Martin-without-the-leg he was Simon-without-a-mother, and, like Martin, he would have to adapt his life-style and not be too sensitive about his handicap. "My mother has died," he practised to himself and then, in answer to imagined questions like, "Have a good holiday, Simon?" he'd say, "Not the best two weeks of my life. My mother died rather suddenly." 'Mother' was the word to use, not 'Mum'. It distanced it, sounded suitably factual and impersonal. Everyone had a 'mother' who could just as easily be lost. 'Mother' was a concept, a label for an idea. He could handle ideas. "Yes," he'd say. "It's been a difficult time but it happens to all of us sooner or later." He approached the little group at the bus-stop with only moderate unease.

He was fairly early and they were all youngsters, four or five first-years and two second-year girls, Sam and her friend.

"Hello," he said and Sam smiled and blushed hotly. The friend looked at the floor. Nobody else spoke. Now and again he noticed the little ones snatching sidelong glances but mostly he watched the traffic passing, and silently cursed Kevin for not being there. He could have called for him. The necessary detour would have been better than this painful limelight. As soon as he recognised Kev's bulky shape advancing he went to meet him gratefully.

"Morning, Simon, my boy," he grinned, as normal as you like.

"Morning, old son." They ambled on, side by side. "Thanks for coming round, by the way."

"What are friends for, mate? Glad to be of service."

"I'm a bit scared about today," Simon confessed.

"Don't worry. We'll get through it," said Kevin and Simon realised that the two of them, together, probably would.

By morning break Simon was certain that he would not be forced to explain to anyone and the great cloud of dread seemed to be dissolving little by little. Either he had the news branded across his forehead or Kevin had been right. He wondered what the notice in the staff room said. 'Simon Walters has lost his mother'?

"Always was a careless lad, that one!"

'Simon Walters – Handle with Care! Mother deceased'?

His form teacher pretended nothing had happened all through registration, checking for absences, giving out notices, calling his name quite normally. Only as they were filing out did she smile straight at him and say, "Glad to see you back, Simon."

He nodded his head and continued on his way. He was doing it all the time these days, as an alternative to speaking. When they were little and had pulled faces, kids used to say, "You'll go like it!" He considered the possibility of 'going like it', wandering round for ever more like a little nodding dog, the sort people put on back window ledges of cars. Supposing his neck muscles went all floppy and he found he couldn't hold his head still? He'd have to agree to everything for the rest of his life.

"Watcha, Si!" called Paul Carter as he shoved his way in the opposite direction. Simon nodded automatically and then grinned to himself. He'd really have to be careful. For the rest of the day he'd practise holding his head up high and replying properly to people, even teachers. When Shylock caught his glance and quickly looked away, Simon made a point of speaking.

"Good morning, sir." The tiny rodent eyes peered somewhere in the region of Simon's tie. "Ah, good morning, er...Walters," he mumbled and hurried on. It suddenly became clear to Simon that he had control – just as he had when he had quite deliberately shocked Kevin on the phone – and that other people were more disconcerted than he was.

Later in the day the fact was brought home to him even more forcibly. They had a French lesson and Miss Craig gave them an old test paper for translation practice. She was very young and inexperienced but Simon liked her because she was keen and hardworking, and although they could easily embarrass or sidetrack her she did her best to give them a fair deal. The lesson began well with an old joke. She talked to them in French and began, as usual, "*Alors, la classe...*"

"Allaw," they chanted, like circus clowns, and waved their little hands back at her. She'd been very surprised when they first did it but this time she laughed happily. Any rapport is better than none, thought Simon. She must have been thinking kindly of him because she asked him to translate the easy bit, knowing he could do it and trying to involve him. It was a little story about a picnic with lots of 'food' words and 'family' words. These French families always seemed to take aunts, cousins, godmothers and great uncles wherever they went, just to test the vocabulary of English school children. The little girl, Maxine, was being difficult because she couldn't find the butter. "'*Le beurre est dans le panier,*' *dit Madame Distel.* '*Le voici! Qu'est ce que tu ferais sans ta maman?*'" He was pleased to have noticed the tense. "'What *would* you do without your mother?'" He looked up for approval. Miss Craig was quite obviously horrified. Her neck was scarlet with embarrassment. She's not prepared this, thought Simon. She didn't know it was coming.

"*Merci, Simon*," she said, pronouncing it the French way. "*Très bien! Daniel?*" Dan Jamieson continued with the text, stumbling clumsily over the words. Several sets of curious eyes were turned on Simon and he was suddenly angry with the silly woman for creating this moment, for putting him on the spot in this way. He looked down at the book, concentrating hard but unable to stop the blush, equally dramatic as hers had been, from flooding upwards. It was his worst moment of humiliation and not his fault at all.

The English lesson, by contrast, proved to be constructively relevant. By accident (Simon could hardly believe it had been planned) the topic seemed entirely appropriate. Mrs. Davies was a strange old bird, given to peasant-style clothes and dangly ear-rings, but she loved literature and the very sound of words, which she delivered in a lilting Welsh accent which they copied without mercy or malice.

"I've brought you a picture," she announced, struggling with a large set of poetry books. "I want you to look at the picture and write down everything that comes into your mind. Give them out, Kevin and Michael. Page thirty-six. You've got two minutes."

"I thought we were doing Ted Hughes this term," said creepy Mary. "I've bought *River* and got *Crow* from the library."

"We are," said Mrs. Davies. "But first we're looking at a picture." By now most of the class had pens poised and were waiting for inspiration to leap up from the rather boring black and white photograph of a landscape that spanned pages thirty-six and thirty-seven.

"What page did you say?" asked Simon.

"Thirty-six."

They were fairly used to this 'brainstorming' exercise in English. There were three possibilities. You could come up with what she wanted, miss the point completely or think of something she hadn't considered at all but which she'd praise excitedly. Her favourite words were 'sensitive' and 'perceptive'. She never dealt in absolutes. You couldn't get nine out of ten or B+ from Mrs. Davies, but you could get 'Well done. Remarkably perceptive', though she never explained why it was remarkably so. Simon tended to assume that it was remarkable considering how mediocre his work was normally. He'd once asked creepy Mary what had been written in her book. "Surprisingly sensitive," said Mary. "She must think it's way above average for this age-group, I suppose."

"Or for you," retorted Simon and left her to ponder.

The book was a paperback and determined to close itself so he rested his left arm across the bottom edge to hold it open. There seemed to be little of any significance to comment on but she wouldn't give it to them if it were really as dull as it looked. There was a ship or two in a bay and up high, on the cliff top, a man ploughing a field, right in the foreground. The shoreline was rocky and there was a faint outline of a city in the distance and an island with what looked like a ruined fort. There was a shepherd and some sheep.

"One minute."

He hadn't written anything. What was important here?

'Ship', he wrote. 'Out to sea'. The billowing sail indicated that it was moving away from the land. 'Farmer. Ancient wooden plough.' The farmer seemed to be watching the blade scything through the turf. The shepherd had his back to the sea. In a flash Simon saw a connection. These men were absorbed with their lives on the land, not watching or caring about the voyaging ship or the distant city. 'Narrow existence', he wrote. 'Lack of vision'. He was pleased with himself.

"Right," she said. "Now who knows who painted this picture?"

"I've definitely seen it before," piped Mary. "It's quite famous, isn't it?"

"Quite famous," Mrs. Davies said, suggesting that it wasn't really. They all liked the way she wasn't impressed by creepy Mary. "It's by Pieter Brueghel. I'll tell you what it is called in a moment."

"Tell us now," grinned Kevin, ever anxious to save himself having to think.

"Tell me what you've written first."

"Not a lot!"

"What have you put?"

"Man in a skirt ploughing. Sheep falling off a cliff. Shepherd doesn't care." Someone giggled.

"What about you, Jane?"

"I haven't written anything yet, Miss."

"Simon?" He felt his idea seemed pretentious now and toned it down a bit.

"The men, the ploughman and the shepherd, don't seem interested in the ships. . .or each other."

"Anyone else? Jane?"

"What's that sticking out of the water, Miss, just below the ship?" Simon was bewildered but then, by moving his arm, he revealed what looked like a white leg protruding from the water. It was either a very large leg or a very tiny ship, he thought.

"Well done, Jane. That's the whole point."

"Very perceptive," said Kevin in his Gareth Edwards voice. Mrs. Davies smiled good-naturedly.

"The painting is called 'The Fall of Icarus'. What do you know about Icarus?" Creepy Mary knew it all. Icarus, she said, had made wings from wax and feathers but had been warned to be careful and not to fly near the sun. He and his father had set off, flying like birds with their great wings until Icarus, growing too confident, had flown too high. The sun melted the wax, the wings collapsed and Icarus crashed to his death.

"When was this?" asked desperate Dan.

"It's a Greek myth, stupid," snorted Mary.

"Liquorice who?" asked Kevin.

"Oh shut up," she whined.

Mrs. Davies had by this time positioned herself on the corner of her desk, feet on a chair. It was her reading pose. She was about to read to them. It was a poem about the picture and though Simon couldn't remember any lines afterwards, except that the ship 'sailed calmly on', he had grasped the message. Tragedies, like the death of Icarus, can happen almost unnoticed while the rest of the world is busy minding its own business.

At the end of the lesson he slipped the book into his

bag, intending to ask his dad to photocopy the picture at work, but then he noticed she was counting the copies. He took it to the front instead.

"Could I possibly borrow the book for a few days?" he asked.

"Why's that, Simon?"

"I'd like a photocopy of the picture."

"If that's all I can do you one now, if you walk down to the staff room with me, providing the machine isn't on the blink." He followed her self-consciously as she swayed down the stairs, her bra strap shining through the back of her flimsy shirt. She looked fat and ungainly from the back. When she came back with the picture for him she was smiling and co-operative. She looked ten years younger from the front. "It's very faint," she said. "I should go to the library and find a better copy. I've written his name on the back for you."

The copy was faint, hardly worth pinning up on his wall at all, but then he began to like it that way, all vague and wishy-washy, as if coming to him through the mists of time. Later, one wet lunch-time, he did go to the library and look up Brueghel. Most of the paintings were fascinating, busy with horrific detail, nightmarish in fact. He was appalled and for many days afterwards wished he'd never heard of the man. However, the Icarus painting stayed on the wall for months, reminding him not to be too angry as the rest of the world ground on relentlessly.

Having got through the day without too many difficulties, he was not prepared for the shock of the empty house. It was as silent and eerie as it had been that day, but there was no shopping in the kitchen, just a note from Suzie saying, 'Take care, both of you. I'll keep in touch. Much love, S.' It was propped against a cast-iron casserole which she had told him to heat up for the evening meal. A glance inside turned his stomach. It was full to the top with what he assumed were vegetables and chunks of meat but the grease had coagulated into a revolting skin. What was he supposed to do with it? He'd seen her preparing it on the hotplate but she'd said something about the oven. He lifted it towards the oven, surprised by its weight, then had to put it down again before he could open the oven door. It wouldn't go in until he'd rearranged the metal shelves but once it was safely in he reached for the knob. He hadn't a clue what heat he needed. He was useless! His search through the recipe books was hampered by the blurring of a few tears which he wiped away angrily with the back of his hand.

If you can't cope with a casserole, heaven help you, he thought. A section on reheating meat told him that it could be dangerous unless it was done thoroughly so he turned the knob up to its highest heat and decided to check it later. Dad would be home between half-past six and seven. He'd got at least two hours to kill.

He thought of phoning Kevin but having only just left him at the bus-stop it seemed a bit silly. Anyway, he couldn't rely on one person all the time. He made himself a mug of coffee, found a few biscuits and padded off to his room. He could always do some homework, either the French exercise or the poem for English. He hated writing poems. It seemed so pointless, writing a poem to order. It would be different if he had some burning message to convey but usually he found himself with a blank sheet of paper and no ideas.

He dumped his bag on the bed then moved it to the floor, dumping himself in its place. He sipped the coffee and pondered. He'd need a routine. Today was a luxury. Suzie had cleaned and cooked already but sooner or later he'd have to cope. He'd heard Dad and Suzie discussing him when they thought he couldn't hear.

"What are we going to do about Simon?"

"Will you need a housekeeper while I'm away?"

"I don't think so. He's nearly sixteen after all."

Old enough to look after himself, it seemed, but not old enough to be consulted. He didn't feel nearly sixteen. He wanted to stay only fifteen with people to look after him and cook his meals and wash his clothes.

When the front doorbell rang he dashed down, grateful for the company, whoever it might be. It was Mrs. Green from next door. She'd taken to popping round regularly.

"I saw you come home so I knew you'd be in," she explained as she stepped in, as if that were sufficient explanation.

"Come in," said Simon, closing the door behind her.

"Your Suzanne's gone back to college." He wasn't sure whether it was a question or a statement.

"Yes," he said.

"So I thought you might be feeling a bit abandoned. I'm not stopping because I've got pies in the oven but if you'd like to pop round in about half an hour you can pick one up for you and your dad. I always do a big bake on Mondays."

"Yes, thanks," he said, not expecting gifts.

"Have you got your casserole in?"

"Yeah. Can't you smell it?" Unmistakable whiffs were wafting down the hall.

"Let's have a look." She trundled into the kitchen. She was remarkably polite for a nosy neighbour. "I should turn it down a bit, love. Start high but always turn it down if it's going to be in a while. It'll be nice for your dad then." She opened the oven door and a cloud of smoke billowed into her face.

"Oh no!" he gasped.

"It's alright. Boiled over a touch, that's all. Nothing to worry about." She closed the door and turned the knob down to 150. He noted the setting. "Right, I'll be off. See you in a bit. I'll make a pot of tea."

He was just about to open the door for her when the phone rang. It was Grandma, checking he was OK. She sounded like his mum on the phone and he wanted to keep her talking until he'd memorised the tone and intonation.

"Must go, dear," she said. "I'll keep in touch. Bye."

"Bye," he answered and held on to the receiver even after he had heard her replace the phone. He'd almost forgotten Mrs. Green until she spoke.

"I expect that was your Gran wasn't it, making sure that

you were alright?" Simon wondered if she were psychic or merely blessed with excellent hearing. "She said she'd ring tonight after your first day back." He must have looked bewildered because she added, rather sheepishly he felt, "She phoned me earlier to find out what time you usually got in." He felt invaded, under surveillance.

"Shall I let you out?" he said and then, to soften the blow, "This door can be a bit stiff sometimes."

He watched her waddle down the path. She was very kind. Mum had liked her but that didn't mean she had to take over. She waved as she turned into her own drive then tapped her watch and mimed the drinking of tea. He shut the door and leaned against it. The house was his sanctuary. He had pulled up the drawbridge. He could stay here, rattling around in the empty rooms, or he could toddle round next door and play the grateful child, accepting sympathy and a pie. He looked at the phone but it stayed obstinately silent. There was nobody else likely to call him. He wondered where Suzie was at that moment, what his dad might be doing. Wherever they were he envied them their alternatives. They had to be better than his.

Chapter FOUR

It was possible to look back on it, months later, with a mixture of pride and amazement. He was always glad that he had conducted himself well during those early public performances, that he had been able to prepare himself adequately for the big moments. He could never have faced people again if he had raged in church or sobbed in school. However, the idea that the worst would soon be over, that he could negotiate the big hurdles to be home and dry, had been a miscalculation of colossal proportions. It had nursed him through those early days but had not prepared him for wave upon wave of little horrors which eroded, grain by grain, all that was left of his confidence.

Waking up in the morning was always painful. He would lie there, his limbs like dough, and consciously prime himself until, with a surge of sheer will-power, he could heave out of bed. Once he was up the desire to dive back again, to bury himself under the bedclothes, was almost overpowering. A couple of times he succumbed and involved himself in lies and forged absence notes. Nobody probed too deeply at school though Simon had found himself quite prepared to elaborate on the hastily scribbled message. It was the thought of his dad finding out, and the inevitable confrontation, that stopped the trend.

"We have to go on, Simon. Somehow we have to make ourselves go on or nothing is worth anything any more." That's about it, Simon had thought, but then there was the punch, or crunch, line. "All those years your mother loved and supported this family, we owe it to her." And so getting up and going to school had become a kind of acknowledgement of the standards she had set. He'd learnt to move from bed to bathroom to dressing himself without pause for thought or weakness. Once dressed it was downstairs to a silent breakfast and the clearing of dishes, Dad's and his own. To shut the door behind him as he left the house was both a relief and an anxiety. He'd test it, with a push, to make sure it was locked. He felt responsible.

The worst mornings were those when he woke slowly. The sound of his father leaving, at about twenty past seven, and the starting of the car would drag him out of sleep, and he'd know that soon his tea would arrive and she'd say, as she opened the curtains, "Come on, Sleeping Beauty. It's a lovely, sunny day," or, maybe, if it wasn't, "Get the boat out, Sunshine. We're afloat."

He'd lie there waiting, warm and safe, until he suddenly remembered. It was like a plug being pulled somewhere inside him. A great rush of all that was airy and light emptied and evaporated, leaving a leaden shell in the bed that couldn't stir. It hadn't happened often. He'd once heard his great gran say, "God gives you as much as you can take and no more."

He hated the times in school when other kids moaned about their mothers who – quite sensibly, it seemed to him now – insisted on their offspring being home by eleven or demanded help with jobs around the house. He wanted to shake them, to shout at them for not valuing what they had and he hated to see himself, as he had been, mirrored in them. Several times a day, or so it seemed, he was catapulted into memories, with all their jagged edges, of things he'd said, things he'd done or not done, lost opportunities. It was the raw impossibility of saying he was sorry, of retracting, that undermined every day. Like that day, when he rushed off to school without seeing her. If he had and she'd looked really ill he might not have gone. At first he'd accepted the doctor's verdict, that there was nothing anyone could have done. He'd looked up the details in an encyclopaedia of home medicine to confirm it but couldn't find much. Yet as Suzie questioned him, over and over again, about that day and then about the preceding days, he'd begun to wonder. Had he precipitated the moment by doing, or more likely by not doing, some little thing?

"If only I'd been here," Suzie had said to him.

"Brought her back to life, would you? Sorry I couldn't manage that!" he'd flared.

"No, I didn't mean...I meant if I'd been here I might have noticed, before, you know...if she wasn't well."

"We were here and we didn't know." He'd been so angry at her suggestion that they'd failed her, he and Dad, that he'd shut himself in his room and not come out for hours. He'd done his best. The doctor had said he'd been very sensible. How dare she say that he hadn't!

Now he could distance himself a little he could see it all more clearly. Suzie not only felt guilty for not being there but couldn't believe that they had not been aware of any changes in Mum. He too had raged inwardly against his dad, who'd seen her that morning, been with her all night, yet still gone off to work. Why shouldn't they be angry with him? He'd gone to school without seeing whether she needed him. He'd come home and found her. They'd left the ball in his court. It had been his responsibility. And what had he done? Nothing, except ruin his shoes and smash a bottle of milk.

He was trying to piece together those last weeks, looking for hints or signs that should have warned him, moments he'd overlooked. It was important to get it right, all in the right order, and he found himself snapping irritably at people who interrupted him just as a scene was falling into place. Far from concentrating on school work he found himself living inside his head, where all the good days were, moving inexorably on from minute to minute, breathing in and breathing out, going through the motions.

"Where's your homework, Simon?" Mrs. Davies asked as she moved along the aisles collecting essays.

"Homework?" Not only had he not done it, he couldn't recollect any knowledge of it. "What was it?" he hissed at Kevin as she moved away.

"Ted Hughes essay."

"Oh yes." He remembered the poems, lesson after lesson of them. He'd liked some of them, about the co-existence of beauty and horror and the idea that all living things struggled in vain, but he wasn't sure about the worth of the struggle. Why hadn't he done this essay? "Was I absent?" he asked Kevin.

"When are you not, my boy?" Kev grinned at him. "I'll give you the title later. Tell her you've forgotten it." She asked him to stay behind at the end.

"I've forgotten the essay, Miss. I'll bring it to the next lesson." She looked at him steadily with her this-is-more-in-sorrow-than-in-anger look. "I will do it, Miss, honestly." She hesitated. Choosing her words, he thought.

"Look, Simon, I know it's not easy at the moment but you must know that your whole future depends on what you do now. You mustn't throw it all away." He stood, silent and resentful. If the silly cow couldn't see how stupid that sounded, when he'd already thrown it all away, then he wasn't going to spell it out for her. "Do you need some help to get started?" He shrugged. How could he answer that when he hadn't even thought about it yet. "Do you intend to try?" She was pushing him.

"I am trying!" It came out angry, threatening. She got that message.

"OK. I'll leave you to it. Soon as you can now." He strode away. He'd get the title from Kev and have a go, he'd decided. Anything to keep the nagging at bay! He'd had the same thought, he realised, time without number, whenever his mum had asked him to do things. She'd used the same tactic too, the nag to stir his conscience and then the time-lag while she left him to respond under his own steam, usually late but seldom never. Well, that crappy English teacher needn't expect the same reaction. He'd do it in his own good time, if at all.

And as for Mrs. Green from next door, she'd been manipulating him too, dropping in most nights when he got home from school, often with a cake or some shopping or one of her apple pies that Dad always raved about. Simon began to suspect she'd been put up to it, by Dad or Suzie, to check on him. Didn't they trust him? One night he'd said to her, very politely, "I'm sure you're busy at home. There's really no need to waste time on me. I'm quite capable, in spite of what people say," and he'd smiled, as if he'd meant it as a joke.

"It's no trouble, Simon. I like to see you safely in. Your mum always used to say, 'Must go, Betty. Simon'll be home soon. I like to know he's safely home,' and she'd rush back. I do it for your mum really. But, if you'd rather I didn't..."

"No, I don't mind. I was thinking of you." He was appalled at the ease of the lie. "I don't want to be a nuisance."

"Well, that's one thing you're not, young man. I've never known anyone your age so quiet. Still, you can always pop round if you need me," and she'd let herself out, still smiling cheerfully. It was all over in a few seconds but he'd successfully ensured that he had the silent, empty house entirely to himself for a couple of hours every evening, which was not exactly what he'd intended.

Mrs. Green still came in regularly with food but she let herself in during the day and left her burnt offerings on the kitchen table, not that they were really burnt. Usually they were much appreciated, though she did have a rather strange idea of what constituted soup. She'd also tidy up rather than step over things. He'd know as soon as he opened the door and found the hall tidy that she'd been in. If she hadn't he would know he'd have to start the meal from scratch and he'd feel irritated with her. Then there was a week when she didn't come at all.

"I see Mrs. Next-Door's given up on us," he said to his father.

"Not for good, I hope," Dad said. "Marilyn's here with the new baby this week. You can't expect her to leave them to keep trotting round here. She doesn't see them often enough as it is." It was perfectly understandable. When it came to the crunch, any mother would put her own family first. He'd got to learn not to expect to come first with anyone, except maybe Dad, and then only as long as Suzie was away.

Marilyn, however, did come round on the Saturday morning. He looked her up and down with a growing surge of approval and disbelief, and was amused to see his dad doing exactly the same.

"Hello, Mr. Walters. I've just popped round to see if you need anything, and to say hello of course. Mum and I are going shopping."

"Well, look at you!" said his father. "Motherhood suits you, obviously."

"All diet and hair dye," she said, pleased by his approval, "and young Thomas keeps me busy."

"So where is he? Aren't we going to see him?"

"He's asleep at the moment. Why don't you pop round this evening before I put him to bed?"

"Yes, I'd like that, wouldn't we, Simon?" (So I am at least an afterthought, Simon realised.) "And where's that lucky husband of yours?" Yeuk! How could he? It was like a line from a third-rate movie, but Marilyn, now blonde as well as dumb, didn't seem to notice.

"He's working abroad, in Italy, for a couple of weeks so I thought I'd come and stay with Mum, and Dad of course, for a few days." Simon's dad was still smiling inanely.

"Good idea, too," he said.

"What about you, Mr. Walters? Are you coping? Mum told me all about it. I'm ever so sorry."

"Yes, we're coping, aren't we, son?" Dad drew him close with an arm around his shoulder.

When Marilyn had gone, clicking down the path in her silly high-heels, Simon suddenly said, "I can never do that, can I?"

"Do what?"

"Come home to my mum." There was an awful moment as he wished it unsaid, before his dad answered.

"This will always be your home, son." He should have rushed to him then, hugged his dad and made it alright again but he hesitated. His dad turned abruptly and left the room.

He seemed to be doing a fine job of putting the knife in: teachers, friends, Mrs. Green and now even his dad; a magnet repelling like-poles, he'd lurched through the weeks creating space around himself.

"You should go out more, see friends," his dad had said.

"Like you, you mean? You don't have to feel guilty when you go out. I'm alright on my own."

"At least I'm trying not to lose touch with everyone."

"And I am?"

"I don't know. I don't know what you're trying to do."

"I've got work to do in the evenings. Homework. Surely you've heard of homework?"

"So when did you last do a good piece of homework?"

"I'm always doing it."

"So why do I get letters from headmasters telling me you're not?"

"What does he know?"

"He knows what people tell him and what they tell him is that Simon Walters hasn't done a damn thing for weeks."

"And I suppose you're doing really well at work now you've got nothing else to worry about."

"Now you're being ridiculous."

"OK. I'm ridiculous."

In a perverse way Simon enjoyed these exchanges with his father. The moment of turning defence into attack had to be finely judged. One minute you were on solid ground and then really in the mire and then out again, watching the other one flounder.

"I didn't say you were ridiculous. I said you were being ridiculous, which isn't the same thing."

"Isn't 'were' the past tense of the verb 'to be'?"

"I dare say it is but as you're so clever perhaps you might take a long, hard look at yourself." Simon had rushed to the mirror, peered earnestly at his reflection, pulled a few faces and gasped with horror.

"Ahh! It's me!"

His father had stormed out in disgust. Simon hadn't felt good about it. He knew when he'd gone too far. At least that was a point in his favour.

One person he tried hard not to alienate was Kev who had stuck by him and asked nothing. Kev had been round to the house many times and they'd discussed all manner of things for hour after hour, everything except the one thing that shaped Simon's thinking. Kev had invited him out, to parties, discos, the cinema, fishing, anywhere Kev was going. Sometimes Simon went. Usually he didn't. When others, like Jackie or Sarah, or Pete, Mike and Jed, tried to persuade him, it was Kev who rescued him and supported his arguments, but even elastic has a breaking point. Simon sensed that if he went on refusing, being obstinate, Kevin would call it a day.

So, one Friday evening when Kev phoned to say, "We're off to the cinema. We'll pick you up at six-fifteen, OK?" Simon had said OK. He showered and dressed carefully, sprayed himself with deodorant and scrubbed his teeth. He was glad he had. 'We' turned out to be Kevin, Jackie and Sandy. He was clearly meant to be half of a pair. Sandy was in the front with her mum, who was obviously chauffeuring. Simon squeezed in the back with Kev and Jackie.

"Hi," said Kev.

"Hello, stranger," Jackie squeaked excitedly. "Nice to have you back in circulation. Ouch!" Kev had elbowed her in the ribs.

"This is my mum," said Sandy. "Jackie's dad is fetching us back." The car pulled away and he was trapped.

They queued for a while outside the cinema and Kevin kept the girls happy with a stream of unlikely stories. Simon smiled encouragingly and even laughed genuinely at the thought of Miss Craig being shut in the stock cupboard with Kevin. He'd followed her in to get some books and Mike had shut the door and locked it with the key she'd so thoughtfully left in the lock. After a couple of minutes their banging had alarmed the class who'd been compelled to let them out before official reinforcements arrived, but Kevin had emerged with his tie and shirt undone, wiping his brow and faking exhaustion. The whole class had erupted while Miss Craig turned beetroot.

"But it suddenly seemed a bit cruel so I apologised and admitted I was only joking," he said.

"What did she say?"

"She said she was so embarrassed because not many men could emerge from her cupboard still standing up. That brought the house down. Then the Head appeared, obviously irritated that any class should be having fun in his hearing. 'Is everything alright, Miss Craig?' he said. The whole room went silent. 'Yes, of course,' she said. He must have heard us all sigh with relief, all at once, but he went away." Kev paused. "She's alright, old Craigie!"

"Old Craigie? She's only about twenty-two," Jackie reminded him.

"Past her best, me dear," Kev said, grabbing her to him. "I likes 'em young and tasty." Jackie giggled but showed no sign of struggling.

So Sandy's mine, thought Simon.

Inside the cinema it was warm and dark and Simon relaxed a little.

"It's supposed to be a good film," he told Sandy.

"I know. I've seen it," she said.

"So why come again?"

"It's alright. I don't mind seeing it again." Wonderful! he thought. I've been set up with a girl who's seen the film already. Well, she'll just have to watch it twice.

Next to her Kev and Jackie were already well away and

the main feature hadn't even begun.

"It doesn't take those two long, does it?" he said. Sandy turned around to look, feigning ignorance. She couldn't have not known.

She leaned back towards him and explained, "It's alright. I didn't come for that." Heaven be praised, he thought, and took her hand in gratitude. She squeezed it and sat back, quite content, whispering, "I'm just glad you came." He could feel her smiling at him through the darkness.

"So am I," he lied, wishing Kevin could control himself and watch the screen he'd paid to see. It was very uncomfortable, being next to them when you weren't doing it yourself. He leaned towards Sandy. She smelt lemony and clean. "I won't be long," he said. "Don't go away. I'm just going to make a phone call."

He dashed to the foyer, looking around frantically. People were still paying to get in and the cashier seemed harassed. There was a crush around the sweet counter. Eventually he went back up the stairs to the girl on the door he'd just come out of.

"Is there a telephone I could use?"

"Down the stairs and behind the ticket office," she said, still tearing tickets as people filed in. He ran down again. A girl was using the phone, giving somebody hell about not turning up. "Come on, come on," he chanted to himself. He stood next to her, making sure she knew what he wanted. She turned her back on him and went on talking but lowering her voice, knowing he was listening. Eventually she hung up, looking daggers at Simon as she moved away.

The receiver was damp and warm from her hand and Simon automatically wiped his own hand on his trousers before settling himself to make the call. He punched out the numbers with a trembling finger. It only rang twice.

"Hello?"

"Dad?"

"Simon! I'm just reading your note."

"You got home alright, then?"

"Yes. No problem. The train was a bit late but that's nothing unusual." The thumping in his chest was beginning to subside.

"Can you get yourself something to eat?"

"Yes, of course."

"I'm at the cinema."

"I know. You said in the note."

"I won't be late."

"OK. Have a good time."

"I'm getting a lift."

"Good. See you later."

"See you."

He heard his father replace the receiver before he put his down. Now he could go back and watch the film. Dad would be there when he got in, probably waiting up for him.

Simon got back to his seat just as the main film began which saved him having to explain.

"Everything alright?" Sandy asked.

"Yeah, fine," he said, settling back. He didn't take her hand again, though he did give her the sweets he'd just bought downstairs. Kevin didn't even come up for air, except when the audience gasped at the sight of an enormous crocodile trying to eat the heroine. It was a good film and Simon enjoyed it, was glad to have seen it.

When they got home Kevin asked to be dropped off outside Simon's house, explaining that he only lived a few doors away. It wasn't strictly true but Simon didn't protest.

"Thanks for the lift, sir," Kevin said.

"Yes," added Simon. "Thanks very much."

The two girls waved, Sandy rather less enthusiastically.

"Good film, that!" Kev said.

"How would you know?" Simon couldn't resist the dig, knowing Kev wouldn't care, and he didn't.

"Missed your chance there, old son."

"I take my time. I'm the strong, silent type."

"You're telling me!"

"There's more to life than nooky, mate."

54

"Course there is, but it's not a bad way of passing the time while you're waiting."

"But it's using people." Simon hadn't meant to be critical. He lightened the tone. "Poor old Jackie."

"Did you hear her complain?"

"No, but..."

"Look, mate. I've never pushed anyone, ever, into anything they didn't want. OK?" Simon believed him.

"I know. But you put yourself around a bit don't you?"

"Sowing me wild oats, I am. Nothing wrong in that."

"No. I s'pose not." It wasn't like him to give in so easily but he wanted to go in and wasn't sure he could keep the banter light and easy. He hadn't wanted to touch Sandy, though she was a good friend and he'd known her for years. She'd understood, or he thought she had, in a way that Kev never could. "I'd better go in now, Kev. Dad's probably waiting up." Lights were on downstairs, welcoming. "Thanks for inviting me. I did enjoy it."

"See ya then, Si."

"See ya, Kev."

When he got in his father was slumped in the armchair, his tie loosened and a glass in his hand.

"Good film?" he asked. He looks tired, thought Simon, tired and forlorn. It was a good word, forlorn. He'd only ever seen it in poems. Nobody used it these days but it came into his head now as the right word.

"Sorry I'm late," Simon said.

"You're not late. Stop fussing."

"Have you been alright?"

"Fine, though the television's got a lot to answer for. Not one decent programme! It's always the same in the summer. How was the film anyway?"

"Great. You ought to see it," and then, remembering the situation, he added, "I don't mind seeing it again."

"Maybe."

"Do you want another drink?" Simon took the empty glass and sniffed it. He was expecting the stench of neat whisky, but he didn't recognise this. "What is it?"

"Soluble aspirin."

"Are you ill?" The thumping began in Simon's chest again.

"Just tired. Bit of a headache." How many times had his mum said that? "It's been a tough day, tough week." Simon knew he should never have gone out, letting him come home to an empty house and no tea. What kind of life was it to be now that he couldn't leave the house?

"I'm sorry. I shouldn't have gone."

"Don't be so silly. Of course you should. You're entitled to a life of your own."

"I'm not silly."

"No, you're not. I only meant that you shouldn't worry. I'm fine. Really."

"You look awful."

"Thank you and goodnight, my son."

"Are you coming to bed?"

"Soon. I'm alright here at the moment."

"Can I get you anything?"

"No." His dad was sitting very still, like you do when your head is pounding and you daren't move.

"Sure?"

"Go to bed, Simon."

Well, so be it. His dad didn't want him around. Everyone is entitled to his own life. Simon made himself a drink and took it straight upstairs. He sat on the edge of the bed, listening. There were no sounds. They were each sitting alone, silent, in separate rooms. If Dad had wanted to talk, he'd have listened. He'd wanted to tell him about the film, about Sandy, perhaps even about Kevin and his half-baked ideas. Was he out of line with his scruples? Was he odd, not wanting to take his chances in the back row?

Well, he'd learnt a few things tonight, about himself and other people. 'No worries!' as the Aussies say. He'd stand on his own two feet from now on. If Mum was all that had held them together they'd have to sink or swim by themselves. She'd taught him a 'French' proverb, '*Pas de lieu Rhône que nous*', and he'd puzzled for ages trying to translate it. Then she'd giggled and told him. "Paddle your own canoe!" So that's what he'd do. He finished the drink, went to the bathroom and got ready for bed. He climbed in, lay there still and tense for a while, then reached up to pull the cord. The light went out. All was silent downstairs.

Chapter FIVE

Of course he hadn't bargained on the likes of Charlie
Barber crashing into his life. Even that day had begun
unexceptionally. It was the first Monday of the autumn
half-term holiday, a damp October morning. He had lingered too long in bed, putting off the moment when he had
to settle down to work, compiling mental lists of his homework backlog, rearranging the order of priorities again and
again. Without sufficient coursework they wouldn't enter
him for some subjects. His dreams of going to college, like
Suzie, would crumble at the first fence. On Friday he'd
made a number of rash promises at school, convincing himself and the teachers that the work would really be done.
Now, this morning, the ground seemed to have shifted
again. He had been overestimating the time available and
his own determination.

By the time he rolled out of bed he felt muzzy-headed
and limp. He needed fresh air and a brisk walk so he
decided to go to the shop for a bag of goodies to help him
through the day. One Maths problem completed equals two
chocolate caramels. Two pages of a literature essay equals
a Crunchie bar or a bag of crisps. In his oldest, comfiest
clothes and his dad's gardening jacket he set out, kicking

the few leaves that had already fallen, amazed at the number of webs that draped the hedges, all grey and sticky. In the sunshine they sparkled, flaunting themselves, reminding people of the shocking and infinite proliferation of spiders, but under heavy skies they reminded him of catacombs or Miss Havisham's eerie halls, dusty and decaying. He found a short stick and twirled it in the webs, gathering them like candy floss, then felt like a vandal. He threw the stick over the hedge and thrust his hands guiltily into his coat pockets, finding an empty seed packet in one and the key to the garden shed in the other. The packet was old and faded. He could just make out the words stamped on the back. 'By SPRING 1985'. The picture showed a cascade of sweet peas in pink, blue, lilac, purple and white. They'd grown them up the back of the garage wall and they'd lasted all summer, it had seemed, reproducing almost as fast as Mum cut them. She'd had them in vases all over the place. They reminded her of weddings, she'd said. They'd reminded Simon of butterflies, delicate, pastel, fluttery creatures clustering on the fragile green stalks, but he hadn't said so. He screwed up the packet and pushed it back into the depths of the pocket. His fingers came up smeared and dusty with dried soil.

He'd expected to meet at least one of his friends but the village seemed to have emptied itself of youth. He crossed the road to avoid batty Nora who was dragging two laden carrier bags up the hill and puffing like a geriatric milkmaid, frowning under a woolly tea-cosy. She had men's socks on, rolled down to meet lace-up shoes, and an expanse of raw leg glared redly for a few inches below the hem of her tweed coat. There was a nip in the air and all her exposed bits reminded him of meat. She revolted him and he marvelled that she was not only married but also had children, with all that the process entailed. If she had once been young and desirable when had the rot set in? At what point in her life had she become bitter, bloated and ugly? If it had been a gradual deterioration did she even know what had happened to her? No wonder the good die young, he thought.

No one under the age of fifty crossed his path. He nodded to Mrs. Green as she drove past him; he appreciated the friendly wave and toot of the horn. He gazed around. A man was trying to start his car in a driveway, leaning into the engine under the raised bonnet and coughing hoarsely and compulsively. A cigarette burned by itself, ledged on the rockery, sending twisty spirals of smoke into the thin grey air. When the man tried to start the car it gave a dry, mocking cough.

Near the shops there was more sign of life. A mother was trying to strap a struggling toddler into a buggy while yelling shrilly at a slightly older clone who was jabbing a finger into a large dog tied to the railings.

"Wayne! Wayne! Come 'ere! It'll bite yer." Wayne was obviously deaf. The dog, a plump and elderly retriever, sat patiently as if being poked was all part of life's tedious pattern.

"Wayne! I'll smack yer if I 'ave to come and get yer." Wayne stepped back a couple of inches. The dog blinked wearily. As the woman stood up straight and moved towards them the buggy, weighted by a bag of shopping, fell backwards and the infant set up a harsh and protracted howl. By the time she'd grabbed Wayne's hand to pull him away Simon had picked up the push-chair and the shopping, noticing with distaste the red mottled face and sticky, runny nose of the pinioned child. The woman, who didn't look much older than the girls at school, grabbed the handle from him. Too embarrassed to thank him she struggled away, covering her awkwardness with a fresh attack on the now shrieking Wayne, tottering her way home in scuffed high-heels. Her legs, pale and spindly, were also bare, emerging like a bird's from the bulk of her clothing and terminating in those huge, dirty-white shoes. Like Olive Oyl's, Simon thought. He was imagining her husband, wondering if he bore any resemblance to Popeye or whether he was small and already defeated, like Wally in *Last of the Summer Wine*. Marry too young and you've lost before you've started, he thought. There was no way he'd ever saddle himself with responsibilities like that before he was about thirty. He felt sorry for the woman – for the girl, for that was all she was – and for the woman she would become, another Nora trapped by self-perpetuating limitations.

Suddenly the dog barked, a deep, throaty friendly sound, and Simon turned to see a man emerge from the green-grocer's and hurry towards it. The dog stood up, tail thumping, body dipping in excitement. The sun, breaking through a cloud, turned its coat to gold, and the man untied it skilfully then cuddled the gleaming head. Simon felt envious and was still watching the dog, its pale fronds glinting as it swayed, as he turned into the doorway of the newsagent's and straight into a full frontal collision.

"Oh, I'm sorry," they both said as a bagful of mint humbugs cascaded over the pavement. The girl bent to pick them up, still clutching a dog's lead in one hand. Simon bent down too, not brave enough to step over her and leave her to it.

"I was watching the dog," she said, glancing towards a small, white, squat little thing that was sniffing eagerly at the scattered sweets.

"So was I!" he answered, nodding towards the retriever which was conveniently trotting past the doorway.

"I like those," the girl said. "I'd have a big dog if my dad would let me, but he won't." Simon handed her half a dozen humbugs then moved away to collect the ones that had bounced furthest.

"I think that's the lot," he said, tipping them into the paper bag that she held open for him.

"Thanks. They're for my gran. She sent me out with a little list. Half a pound of mints or toffees, a *Woman's Own* and don't come back till you've had a good walk!"

"You've forgotten the *Woman's Own*," Simon said as he watched her push the sweets into a pocket. The red anorak she was wearing looked well-worn and old-fashioned without any big pockets that might have concealed a magazine.

"I've got to come back after lunch. They haven't been delivered yet."

"Oh, right," he said. "Anyway, sorry about all that." He went in and took his time choosing, still flustered by the memory of her body against his and the shock of the moment. He hadn't taken in enough detail to bring her to mind easily, except for the scruffy red coat and the voice. Her accent was different, though he didn't recognise it. He'd certainly never met her before.

"You want to be careful, Simon Walters. Fancy a big lad like you knocking over a little thing like that!" It was Maureen, from school. She was wearing a pink nylon over-all and was flicking a duster across the book displays.

"Hello. What are you doing here?"

"Working. It's a holiday job. I'm going to do it on Saturdays, too."

"Whatever turns you on!"

"Don't be rude," she said, flicking him with the duster. "I need the money."

"Don't we all."

"So why aren't you working?"

"No time," he said. "I've got six months' homework to do this week."

"So why aren't you doing it?"

"I'm working up to it."

"Sandy says you're a slow starter."

"Does she?"

"But worth waiting for."

"How would she know?"

"You tell me!"

Simon tapped his nose and winked.

"Come on, I'll ring those up for you unless you're shop-lifting."

"Who, me?" He handed her the money. "Can I have a bag please, so I don't drop them." She gave him a small white bag that only just held everything.

"You'll get fat," she said.

"Cuddly," he corrected.

"I finish here at six," she teased.

"I told you, I'm working." He grinned. He liked Maureen. She was stick-like and flat-chested, with straight mousy hair that hung in lank curtains, but she was friendly and kind. Nobody asked her out on dates but everyone, even the boys, told her their troubles. She made jokes against herself so no one else had to do it. "I'll be burning the midnight oil all week if I don't get started soon."

"Then you'll need me to keep your little lamp burning. I could trim your wick."

"You could get the sack. Old Troutface is watching us. Wave your duster or something." Maureen smiled and then, raising her voice, dismissed him efficiently.

"Will that be all, Mr. Walters? Right. Thank you for your custom. Do call again. Have a nice day!"

"Don't overdo it," Simon hissed. "He may be ugly but he's not stupid," and then, louder, "See ya, Mo. I'll phone maybe." Maybe he would. She was one of the nicest people he knew.

By the time he came out the sun had painted everything in brighter colours and the red coat hit him straight in the eyes. She was stooping awkwardly in the middle of the pavement, fondling the dog, while people had to walk round her. An old lady, trailing an ancient shopper on wheels, tutted critically as she had to change course. The girl looked up, saw him and stood up eagerly.

"You were ages," she said. "What were you doing, buying up the stock?"

"Only half of it," he said. "It's my reward system. I pay myself in things that are bad for me but enjoyable, as a reward for doing work that is good for me but horrible."

"What kind of work?"

"G.C.S.E. coursework."

"Oh, poor you! Is it awful? I was lucky. I did O-levels." He looked down at her. It was hard to believe she was older than him, though faces could be deceptive.

"When?" he asked.

"Last year. This year, I mean. In June."

"How did you do?"

"OK."

"How many did you pass?"

"All of them, thank goodness. At least it kept Dad quiet."

"How many is all of them?" She seemed to hesitate. Is she lying, Simon wondered.

"Eleven," she said.

"Eleven!"

"I hate telling people," she explained. "Everybody thinks I'm a creep or a genius or something. People usually take a step backwards."

"So," Simon said. "Who's right? Are you a creep or a genius?" She looked hurt, as if she'd known he'd react like this but hoped he wouldn't. "I'm sorry," he added. "I don't mean it. You look quite normal from the outside."

"I did English, Maths and French early," she said, "in the fourth year, and the rest in the fifth."

"Genius," he decided. She punched him playfully. People were still having to walk round them and the little dog was pulling, scampering in front of people and getting in the way. It wasn't until a little boy fell over the taut lead that she decided to move. She picked up the dog and moved back against the shop window while Simon picked up the second child of the morning. He was about four and obviously used to mishaps. He didn't cry but jerked angrily to free himself and raced back to where his mother was gossiping with a friend. The two women continued, unaware of the accident, for which Simon felt truly grateful.

The girl obviously didn't intend to let him go easily.

"I was wondering," she said, "if you could advise me. Where can I take this monster for a walk and let him off the lead safely?"

"Up on the downs, I should think. He'll be safe up there." The monster, as she'd called him, was obviously used to being cuddled. He lay like a baby in her arms, his head lolling backwards, his bright button eyes watching

Simon's every move. "What's his name?" he asked, stretching out a hand to tickle under its chin.

"Robbie," she said, rolling the 'R'. "He's a West Highland Terrier, born in Edinburgh even. Gran brought him back from a holiday. He's got a little coat for winter made out of red tartan."

"To match your coat?" Simon suggested.

"It's Gran's jacket, not mine," she replied. "I wouldn't be seen dead in this back home." She cradled the dog affectionately and then looked up at Simon, smiling. Simon withdrew his hand.

"What makes you think you'd have a choice?" he said.

"Sorry?"

"People don't choose what they're seen dead in." She looked confused.

"No. I suppose not," she said. Simon was staring past her. "Have I said something stupid?" she asked, waiting.

"It doesn't matter," he said, and then, "I'd better go. I've got lots to do."

"OK," she said. "Which way to the downs?"

"Don't you know the village at all?"

"Not really. Only the main bits."

"Along here, turn left at the end and up the lane for a couple of hundred yards. There's a little track down the side of a cottage. Follow it under the railway bridge and it will lead you right up to the top." He pointed towards the end of the parade of shops. She put Robbie down and turned to follow his finger.

"Can you say it again?"

"Left at the end, by the cake shop, and follow the lane. OK?"

"Right."

"No, left." He grinned again. The girl looked relieved.

"Then what?"

"Look for the track by the cottage."

"Which cottage?"

"The one by the track."

"On the right or the left?" He indicated with his hand.

"This side."

"Right."

"Right."

"Under the railway bridge."

"Railway?"

"It isn't there now. There used to be a railway line. It's now a grassy track."

"But there is a bridge?"

"Would it be easier if I showed you?" Simon was beginning to think he'd never get away. She chuckled and the smile went all the way to her eyes which stared quite directly and honestly into his.

"Yes, please," she said.

Together they set off, every step taking him further from his books. Along the lane Simon found himself walking on the inside, nearest to the hedges while the dog, sniffing ecstatically, crossed and re-crossed in front of him, not caring about the lead which threatened to trip him every few steps. The girl apologised a couple of times and then handed him the lead so that Robbie now had free access to the most interesting odours. That left her right hand free and Simon's left hand free. Her sleeve brushed his. He put his spare hand into his pocket and encountered the key again. He ought to have put the sweets in there, instead of the other side, to keep the key safe, but it was too difficult to swap them over now. He ran his fingertips over the smooth metal. It was so tiny, just a padlock key, but so vital. Dad would go mad if he lost it. He'd only worn the coat because it was hanging conveniently over the bannister.

"Why are you wearing your gran's jacket?" he said.

"She likes me to keep warm. I didn't bring what she calls a 'proper coat'."

"You're just visiting then?"

"Mmm. Just this week. Dad's fetching me next Saturday."

"I haven't seen you before."

"I've never stayed here before. Only visited occasionally

and not for ages anyway."

"What do you think of it?"

"Of what?"

"Round here."

"It's pretty."

"Pretty boring."

"That too," she said. Suddenly he felt the need to defend it and was irritated by her quick agreement.

"There are worse places to live," he argued. "Most people would be glad of the chance." He remembered cousin Keith at the funeral, over-enthusiastic about the place. "Imagine driving home along country lanes," he had said, "instead of the м6 in the rush-hour. Imagine opening the windows to hear the birds and smell the country air."

"Oooh, listen to 'im," Auntie Beryl had said. "He'd run a mile from a cow and even the smell of cats makes him cross."

"Only incontinent cats," he'd retorted, looking hard at his mother. But Keith had been quite serious. "When I die," he'd said, "I'd like to be buried in a country churchyard just like this. It seems right. I mean, it's nature innit? You're born, you live, you die and the earth takes you in. Like plants do. Feeding the ground. Natural cycle."

"Shurrup, our Keith." But he wouldn't stop.

"We're not meant to live in towns, race around like crazed rats and then, when we're burnt out, be shoved in an oven 'cause it's quicker."

"So you'll be moving to the country, then?" his mother had asked. "What about your job?"

"Stuff that!" he'd said.

"But you've done so well. You can't just leave all that."

"Watch me," he'd said and Auntie Beryl had frowned anxiously and then turned to one of the old ladies.

"He's a one, that lad o' mine. Never know what he's going to do next."

Simon hadn't been sure whether he liked Keith or not. At first he'd seemed good-hearted, brash, an offshoot of his mother, a genuine sort of character. But there had been glimpses of a harder streak, of a will that persisted no matter what. You didn't get to drive a sleek, new Jaguar by being good-natured. Simon could well believe that if Keith made up his mind to do something he'd do it, regardless of the consequences.

They'd reached the track.

"Some people," said Simon, "like the countryside and a village isn't as impersonal as a town or city."

"Nor as exciting," she said. "But actually, I do like it. It's peaceful."

"You can let the dog off the lead now. He'll be alright."

"I couldn't do that in a town."

"Not if you liked the dog."

She set Robbie free and they watched him race away into a green, shadowy world of rustles and hummings and swishes as the wind strengthened. Briefly he would appear in the pathway as he zigzagged in and out of the jungle of bushes and grasses, overwhelmed and undecided, too excited to concentrate on anything.

Simon fastened his jacket and wished he'd been wearing something warmer, like his new ski jacket. The girl turned up the collar of her gran's coat. Either side of them, unseen creatures skittered in the undergrowth, fleeing from their footsteps. It was wet and muddy. He wasn't dressed for this. Only the insects seemed oblivious. A few still danced in shafts of sunlight while the two intruders strode through them. They wouldn't last much longer.

The track curved under the old bridge and then climbed in an almost straight line. Simon stopped and pointed.

"It's easy now. You can follow it all the way up to the Ridgeway if you want to. Make sure you come back the same way."

"Is it safe?"

"Yeah, there's no problem. If you see the racehorses you'd better put the dog on the lead again – but they won't be up there at this time, I shouldn't think."

"I'm not sure about going up there alone." Simon had a

sudden sense of being outplayed. She'd had no intention of going alone, not since she'd decided to wait outside the shop. He wasn't going to make it easy.

"Do you want to call him back then?"

"I don't know if he'll come." Simon looked at his feet. His newest school shoes were wet and caked with mud. The girl's feet were even worse. She'd been wearing canvas trainers which were now saturated and possibly beyond redemption. Her tight black leggings were smeared and splashed. They were at least in fashion but might have looked better on someone else.

"Aren't you cold?" he asked.

"I'm alright on the move," she said. "It's standing still that gets to you."

"What do you want to do?"

"You couldn't come with me, just for half an hour, could you?" Simon wondered how he managed it so often, how he could allow himself to be trapped so consistently by women into doing what they wanted. His mum had been the arch-manipulator, always knowing how to put him back on course, and Suzie too, patient, supportive, relentless. Female teachers, pushing, persuading, casting a motherly eye, made him cough up the work eventually – Bessie, Mrs. Davies, Miss Craig, all so well-meaning. And now this stranger, whom he'd met less than fifteen minutes ago, had got him half-way up a hill he hadn't intended to climb. He shook his head. Her face fell.

"Might as well," he said.

Chapter
SIX

He looked at his watch. "Half an hour you said?"

"Half an hour."

"In fifteen minutes we turn back."

"Fine!"

They set off briskly, occasionally catching glimpses of Robbie as he raced back and forth.

"This is stupid," he said. "You're soaked." It was a walk for warm summer days or wellington boots.

"I'll have a hot bath when I get back. I'll be alright." She didn't seem to want to give up. Perhaps she was lonely. They strode on, warming up with the effort.

"Do you know anyone else round here?" he asked.

"No."

The slope was becoming steeper and more slippery. Once she slid and he had to grab her arm to stop her from falling. It was easier not to talk. When they came to the first crossroads, where a stony track crossed their own, she stopped to look at the view and get her breath back.

"Where do you live?" Simon asked.

"Cheshire, not far from the Welsh border."

"And your gran lives here?"

"Yes."

"Why's that?"

"What do you mean?"

"It's a long way."

"Dad works in Chester so we live near Chester. Gran has always lived down here." He felt guilty of prying and decided to keep quiet but she didn't seem to mind. She answered his questions without being asked. "That's why I don't see much of her and why I decided to come here for half-term. Dad's gone to Geneva, to a conference, and he's picking me up on the way back. Do you know my gran?"

"Don't know! Who is she?"

"Mrs. Hadley. Holly Cottage. It's in Brook Lane, up past the vicarage. Do you know it?"

Simon did. He knew most of the local houses from his bob-a-jobbing days. He cringed inwardly at the memory of his eight-year-old self, spruce in his Cub uniform, earnestly enquiring whether he could do any jobs as he interrupted household after household. He'd once been given some weeding to do at Holly Cottage and had uprooted whole rows of bedding plants before the lady had caught him and stopped him. In the end she'd paid him not to finish the job. That was the year he'd collected the most money in the pack and he'd been really proud. He'd run all the way home to tell everyone and Mum had hugged him and said how well he'd done but Dad had teased him, making jokes about being paid *not* to do jobs, calling it a tidy little protection racket. Suzie had joined in with the joke and they'd kept it going for ages. Weeks later when he'd wanted to help his mum to ice a cake Suzie had said, "Quick, Mum. Give him 10p!" and collapsed into fits of giggles.

"I weeded your gran's garden once," he admitted. "Not very well, though. I hope she doesn't remember."

"I'll ask her. What's your name?"

"Simon. Simon Walters."

They set off again, still trudging upwards. Simon was a few yards ahead of her when he heard her squeal. By the time he turned she was on her hands and knees in a patch of sludge.

"I slipped," she said.

"No kidding!"

For the third time that morning he set someone upright. He waited while she cleaned her hands on the grass and then on her leggings.

"I think it's time to go back," he said. This time she agreed. They scanned the hillside for the dog and then she called him. As if by magic the grass behind her parted and Robbie's little woolly head appeared.

"Hello, Ratbag," she murmured as he bustled into full view, wagging his rear end and waiting for praise. "Time to go." He trotted obediently ahead of them on four glistening, muddy feet. They were both concentrating on staying upright and their chosen safe routes took them apart and then brought them back together again just before the bridge.

"You'd better put him back on the lead," Simon advised.

"We'll have to catch him first." She dragged the brown leather lead from her pocket and, seeing it, Robbie trotted back to her, anxious to be attached.

"Well caught!"

"Not very bright, is he?" she grinned.

By the time they got back to the tarmac surface of the lane Simon was beginning to feel self-conscious. He was wet to the knees. She looked muddy all over. What would people think?

"That wasn't the most sensible idea you've ever had," she exclaimed, realising what she looked like.

"Wonderful! You lead me, a complete stranger, up into the hills and then tell me it's my fault."

"Well, you suggested it."

"You didn't have to go."

"You didn't have to come."

"Let's hope no one sees us."

"Why? Is it going to be embarrassing if you're seen with me?" she asked, genuinely concerned.

"No. Of course not. I just meant the state we're in."

"Who cares what other people think?"

"It's alright for you. You don't live here."

"I wouldn't care if I did." Simon believed her. She really was the most confident, forthright girl he'd ever come across.

"What's your name?" he suddenly asked.

"Charlotte. Dad calls me Charlie but with Gran it's always 'Charlotte, my dear'."

"Which do you prefer?"

"Oh, I'm Charlie to everyone else."

"It's not a very feminine name!"

"I can handle that." She could too. Even in an ancient borrowed coat, muddy black leggings, devastated shoes and with dirt-smeared hands and face, she was undoubtedly female.

As they squelched back through the village Simon played the tourist guide.

"That's the house where old Mr. Cooter hanged himself. It's been empty for years but now a young couple have bought it. They're doing it up as a country retreat."

"Don't they mind, about Mr. Cooter I mean?"

"Nobody's told them. It's a village conspiracy. Everybody's waiting to see if his ghost walks to scare them away."

"Do you believe in ghosts?" she asked.

"No." He was decisive, very sure. If it were possible for a dead person to appear, or send messages, his mum would have done so. He'd even sat by the grave a few times, hoping for a sign, but the wound in the earth had healed, sealed itself with grass, and he'd known that wherever she was now, it wasn't here.

They passed an untidy-looking cottage. "That's where my mate Kevin lives. He lives with his mum and two sisters. His dad left three years ago and hasn't been seen since. Kev's gone to Ireland this holiday to see his auntie."

Further down the lane they came to a pretty, tiny cottage with a picture-book well in the front garden. "Marje lives there. One of my mother's friends. When I was little we used to go there for coffee or afternoon tea and I was always scared I'd be pushed down the well. I used to have nightmares about it. I was nine before I dared to go close enough to drop stones in. They only fell a few feet. It's not a real well at all. All those years I'd been terrified to go near it. I felt a right Charlie!"

She thumped him gently on the arm.

"Very funny!" They were almost back to where they started, where the lane met the main road.

"I'll walk back with you," Simon said. "I can go past your gran's and then back home along the bridle path."

"Great!" said Charlie.

They passed the church on the left-hand side and she peered over the wall. "It's very old, isn't it?" The church-yard wall and many of the tombstones were grey and dappled with lichen. There were some too old to read, names once carefully carved but now weathered into oblivion.

"The original church is very old, yes, but they've added so many different bits over the centuries it's hard to imagine what it once looked like. I'm not really keen on churches."

"It's cathedrals I hate," said Charlie. "All that wealth and power posing as the word of God, centuries of injustice and hypocrisy." Simon was surprised at the vehemence of her reaction.

"But it wasn't all bad, surely?"

"No, I know. I don't mean to be so critical. It's just that when you think of the cost of a cathedral, in money, time and effort, it seems incredible – that the church could flaunt its wealth and that people could accept it."

"Think of the work it provided, for ordinary people."

"Think of the harm, the wars, the Inquisition, the guilt that comes from religion."

"Not just Christianity."

"No. I said religion."

"People need something to believe in, surely?"

"What do you believe in, Simon?"

Why was he arguing with her? He agreed with her. He hadn't found the church or religion any comfort. His heart always sank when he saw the shiny black toe-caps and the swinging skirt of the vicar heading towards him, yet essentially the man was kindness itself. If only he could believe in the assurances. He wanted to ask the vicar one day if he really believed all he said to the bereaved, one day when he had the courage.

"Not a lot at the moment," Simon answered.

Just then a bus surged past, its coachwork overhanging the narrow pavement, forcing them both back against the wall. Two astonished faces peered down at them.

"Friends of yours?" Charlie enquired.

"Yes. Sort of. Sandy and Jackie. They're in my form."

"But not your girlfriend or anything?"

"No," said Simon. "Not my girlfriend."

"Do you have one?"

"Hundreds."

"Anyone special?"

"No."

"Thank goodness for that. I'd hate to break up a happy partnership."

Simon wondered if that meant she had further designs on him until she added, blushing, "By being seen with you in this state, I mean."

"What will you say to your gran? Is she likely to mind?"

"No. She's lovely, my gran. She'll order me into a hot bath, make tea and fuss like mad." Simon felt totally bereft. Would anyone ever do that for him again? He began to hurry, feeling the coldness and dampness of his clothes more keenly. Charlie trotted at his side, breaking into a little run now and again to try to keep up with him while Robbie scuffled through the leaves, playful as a little curly lamb. All too soon they reached the barred gate of Holly Cottage, she was through it and he was left on the outside, shut out. She was turning towards him, about to speak, when a voice cut in.

"Charlotte, my dear. There you are. Have you tired him

out?" Charlie winked at Simon.

"I think he's definitely had enough of me for one day, Gran." She dropped the lead and the dog raced to his owner who, seeing the condition he was in, snapped, "Sit!" before he had time to jump up. Robbie sat, head erect, on the doorstep, looking just like the china dog that Simon's grandmother had on her window ledge.

"Come on in," Mrs. Hadley said to her granddaughter. "Just look at you! Wherever did you take him?"

"I'll tell you all about it," Charlie said. She looked back at Simon, or at least he thought she might have done. He was already walking away.

By the time he got home he had walked off some of the rage that had suddenly boiled up inside him. He wasn't angry with Charlie, only with a world that had left him outside looking in. Dad had kept up his outside interests as well as his job, refusing to allow himself time to think. Suzie had not only breezed back to college but also found herself a steady boyfriend who, more than likely, would be his brother-in-law before long. She'd even brought him home for part of the summer holiday and he'd shown interest in Dad's ideas and done his best to get on with everyone. He was called Bruce and except for his name, which seemed more suited to an Alsatian, Simon had liked him. Even Dad had approved, as much as he was ever likely to approve of anyone who dared to lay hands on Suzie, though Bruce had become noticeably less popular in the last fortnight since Suzie phoned to say she wasn't coming home for half-term. Bruce's Canadian relatives were coming over it seemed, and the whole family, which now included Suzie, would be gathering in the Lake District to meet them.

Simon's half-term was to be devoted to school work all day and his usual evening chores, the shopping, cooking and cleaning-up ritual. Weekends were for cleaning and the 'big shop'. While Charlie went in to a warm fire, no doubt, and grandmotherly fuss, he'd been left outside the gate. After giving up his morning, giving up his precious time, he was going in to an empty house, dirty breakfast dishes, unmade beds and not even a dog to welcome him home.

As he put the key into the front door he reminded himself of one of his mother's much-used epithets. 'It is better to say "I am miserable" than to say that the world is ugly.'

"Well, I am miserable," Simon shouted into the empty hallway. He tramped into the kitchen. "And this bloody kitchen is ugly!"

He was half-way out of his wet jeans when the phone rang. He hopped towards it and lifted the receiver.

"Simon," she said. "Can you come for lunch?"

"What now?"

"When you're ready."

"I don't know. I've got to work, honestly."

"What are you doing at the moment?"

"Shivering," he said. "I've only just got in."

He could hear another voice in the background and then Charlie answering. "He says he's got to work." Then she was back.

"Gran says your work's got to come first and I'm to leave you in peace." He didn't know what to do. Charlie or homework? What kind of a choice was that? When he didn't answer she said, "Can you come for lunch another day?"

"Yes, of course."

"OK. I'll be in touch...and Simon?"

"Yeah?"

"Go and have a hot bath or something straightaway."

"Yeah, alright."

"Bye," she said.

"Bye."

It was all over so quickly. He wanted to phone her back, to say he'd come after all, today, now, but one doesn't do such things, not if one has any sense at all.

But he felt better. What kind of a girl was it who, in the space of about an hour, could make him talk more than he'd talked for months and with one brief phone call make him feel important?

By tea-time he'd cracked the system. The kitchen was clean, the house tidy enough, there was a shepherd's pie in the oven and Mrs. Green, bless her, had popped round with an egg custard which would do for pudding tonight. Best of all, he'd done his Maths assignment for the week which had proved not too difficult once he'd got down to it properly. The only thing he hadn't done was to have the hot bath but Charlie would never need to know that. He'd tell her he had.

He spent another hour sorting out his school bag and cataloguing his workload, this time setting out the list on paper in columns headed 'Essential', 'Desirable' and 'Forget It'. He put Maths in the 'Essential' column and then ticked it proudly. He'd have to do all his English too, or at least two pieces of the missing three, and make some progress with his History project. The Physics he understood so what did it matter if he didn't write up the experiments? He wrote it in the 'Desirable' column and then circled it, with an arrow pointing into the 'Forget It' column. There comes a time when choices have to be made.

He felt satisfied with his first day. At least he'd be clean and tidy when his father came home and with the jobs done there'd be no focus for a row. Tomorrow he'd do one of the English essays. He'd got about half an hour to spare.

Their new 'power shower' had magic properties and he resorted to it frequently. With the water as hot as he could bear and the dial switched to 'massage', he gave his body the treatment and then, turning it down a little and having switched it to 'champagne', he washed his hair and sang his current repertoire. Twenty minutes and many gallons later he emerged, towel around his waist, and headed for the kitchen again. His father was already home, slicing open the morning's crop of bills with a ferocious irritation.

"Hello. You're early," Simon said pleasantly.

"The phone was ringing. Didn't you hear it? The damn thing stopped, just as I got in through the door."

"I was in the shower."

"I don't know who it was. It could have been important." There were times when it was hard to believe that his father wasn't joking. Simon began to fill the kettle.

"Sorry. I'll try not to have showers in future in case the phone might ring."

"There's no need for sarcasm," snapped his father.

How easily they could irritate each other, he thought, but, still mellow after the hot water, Simon decided to try again.

"I've made shepherd's pie. I hope you're hungry."

"What's all this in aid of?"

"You've been to work. I haven't. I thought I'd get the meal organised early, that's all."

"I don't know why your sister couldn't have come home this week. She likes cooking."

There really wasn't any point in trying, was there?

"She's entitled to her own life, Dad."

"And I'm entitled to see my only daughter now and again. Who does she think is paying for this course?"

"You wanted her to do it." His father moved towards the kettle and picked it up. Simon sighed loudly. "What are you doing?"

"Putting the kettle on. What does it look like?"

"I've just done it. You've just seen me do it." He watched his father plug it in again, wearily. He looked faded – greying hair, grey suit, grey-faced. "I'll make some tea while you go and get changed," Simon added.

"Go and put some clothes on first. What happens if someone comes to the door?" The voice was snappy, agitated. Simon tried to lighten the mood.

"Then I'll open the door in my little loin cloth," and he whipped the towel open, shimmied around the kitchen and strode naked down the hall. On his way upstairs he called, "Two sugars please Dad."

Through the open door of the kitchen he saw his father propped against the sink, his weight channelled down two straight arms, his head lowered, defeated. He's tired, Simon thought, and he's miserable. He was glad he'd had a positive afternoon and that the pie smelt good in the oven. If Dad were to say thank you now it would be enough.

When he came back, properly dressed, his dad was pouring the tea into two chunky mugs.

"There's a piece of egg custard too, if you fancy it while you're waiting."

"You haven't made that too!"

"No. Mrs. Green's, I'm afraid. It looks OK though."

"I'll go up and change then. Give me a shout when it's ready."

"Do you want a piece or not?"

"Not at the moment."

Simon watched him take the tea and, without a backward glance, move off to his room upstairs. Sometimes it seemed as if they couldn't bear to be on the same floor, never mind in the same room. Simon began to set the table. It didn't take long with only two place-settings. Then he put some frozen peas into a saucepan to cook. He'd make instant gravy at the last minute, using the soluble granules.

He wondered what Charlie was having for tea. He wondered what he would have had for lunch. He wished himself there, by the fire, with thick toast on a toasting fork and butter and jam. Simon pondered on the power of women to create a home. Without Mum the family had become a sham. She had been the linchpin that held them all locked into the framework. Now, without even Suzie, he felt adrift. Charlie's phone call had lifted his spirits and he'd surged through the afternoon on a wave of optimism. Yet, in five minutes, his father had brought him firmly back to earth.

When he called up the stairs his voice sounded aggressive, even to himself.

"Are you ready yet?"

"As ready as I'll ever be."

In the kitchen he stirred the gravy rhythmically while the heavy footsteps advanced, bringing the storm cloud nearer and nearer. If there was going to be another row he was ready for it. He didn't even turn round until his father spoke.

"Simon," he said. "This looks lovely. Thanks, son."

Chapter SEVEN

By seven o'clock Simon was washing up while his father dried.

"What time will you be back then?" he asked his dad.

"About ten, give or take half an hour."

"When the pubs shut, you mean."

"I suppose we might call in for a quick one."

"What's it tonight then?"

"Badminton Club Committee Meeting." Simon knew exactly what was coming next. "You could join if you wanted to. Do you good."

"Not my scene, Dad! Mind that jug. It's slipping." His father rescued the jug deftly as it slid.

"How about that then? Greased lightning!"

"Not bad for an old man."

"Less of the old man. I could still wipe you off the court."

"And you still wonder why I don't want to join the Badminton Club."

Simon emptied the water away and reached for the towel. His father frowned.

"Aren't you going to clean the sink?"

"Am I?...Yes. I am going to clean the sink." He gazed

speculatively around. "Where's the cleaning stuff?"

"Cupboard underneath. What are you going to do tonight?"

"Clean the sink."

"After you've cleaned the sink."

"Not sure yet. I'm thinking." Dad was already moving away, checking his pockets with little pats like he always did. Mum would have followed him down the hall chanting, "Wallet, house keys, car keys, hanky," and if he was playing she'd go through his kit too. Many's the time she'd said, "Got everything, Mike?"

"Yes. Yes. Stop fussing."

"Racquet?"

"Oh hell! Where is it?"

Simon decided to let him do it for himself. He had to learn to be responsible on his own. Suddenly a new circuit seemed to cut in and his father remembered.

"Have you done any work today?"

"Work?"

"Homework, for school?" Now there was a stupid question: as if he'd say no!

"Yeah. Bits and pieces. Cracked the Maths. Don't worry. I'll get it done."

His father hesitated, clearly trying to decide whether to pursue the topic or not, then weakened.

"OK then. I'll be off. You'll be alright?"

"Fine."

He heard the door slam and the car engine start. Dad was off and here he was, elbow-deep in scouring cream. It was supposed to be the other way round. He continued to scrub, methodically and thoroughly. By the time he finished, the decision would need to have been made. He considered the options: more homework, reading for his Open Study for English, TV or a bicycle ride round the village. He didn't often set out in the dark for a bike ride but the exercise might do him good and he did have lights. There was an easy circular route, up the hill, along the bridle path, down Brook Lane and back through the village to home, or even back the way he'd gone.

He was not quite finished when the doorbell rang.

"Sh...!" Dad had forgotten something again. Simon traipsed along the hall, holding his creamy hands away from him, just managing to turn the catch with his fingertips.

"It's only me," she said. "Are you busy?"

"No. Come in." He stepped back and she squeezed past his upraised arms. She was looking at his hands. "I always answer the door like this, in case it's a Jehovah's Witness."

"What's wrong with Jehovah's Witnesses?"

"Nothing. I just don't want to be one at the moment." He slammed the door shut with his backside. "I'm in the kitchen."

He led her back down the hall and nodded towards a chair. "Have a pew while I finish this."

"Can I help?"

"No, not dressed like that."

She had appeared on the doorstep not straight out of his head but transformed. She was wearing a long red corduroy skirt and red, squashy suede boots. Her coat was brown leather, expensive-looking, over a cream fluffy jumper. She looked about twenty-one and he was scared to death.

"I like your apron," she said.

He'd forgotten he was wearing it. It was one of Mum's, plastic-coated, tasteless. He'd bought it as a birthday present for her when he was about twelve, at an age when he thought the design – a bra and frilly knickers on a curvy torso – amusing. She'd worn it quite a lot before relegating it to a hook on the back of the pantry door. She must have felt silly in it, though not half as silly as he felt now, yet she'd worn it for him. He took it off and hung it up.

"Keeps me dry," he replied. "Now, to what do I owe the pleasure of your company?"

"Do I need a reason?"

"Have you got one?"

"No. Not really."

"Good. Come with me."

It was all he needed, the assurance that she had come because she wanted to, just as he would have gone, he now knew, to cycle up and down past Holly Cottage. He held out his hand and she took it. It felt tiny and cool.

"Where are we going?"

"Absolutely nowhere," he said and trailed her behind him into the lounge. He sat her down in a large armchair near the fireplace. "Now don't go away. Would you like a drink?"

"Not yet." That meant she was planning to stay a while. His heart-rate seemed to accelerate even more. He needed time to think, to calm down.

"I'll make us a fire then. We haven't had a real fire since last winter," he told her, "but it's much nicer than an electric one." He shifted the heavy electric one out of the hearth and out of their way. Charlie sat still, watching him as he came in and out with coal and newspaper, fire-lighters and sticks. Simon concentrated on the pyramid he was building in the grate, suddenly afraid to look at her. He needed to know what he was going to do next, after this; needed to be in control. He'd make coffee and biscuits, he decided. It had all been so easy this morning. Now he felt anxious, uneasy. She looked so grown-up, remote from him.

"I'll make some coffee while you're doing that," she said. He couldn't easily prevent her.

"OK. Yell if you can't find anything."

She took her jacket off and threw it over the back of the chair, then went out. He could hear her pottering about in the kitchen, his kitchen, and he prayed he'd not left any smelly cloths or mouldy bits of cheese around. By the time he'd got the fire going it was almost all done. She was leaning against the sink unit, her back to the window, waiting for the water to boil. He went towards her with coal-black hands outstretched. She grinned and moved quickly sideways to let him get to the sink, leaned across to turn on the tap for him and passed him the soap. When he'd finished washing she was already holding the towel for him. She held on to it while he dried his hands and then put it neatly back over the towel rail.

"You managed to find everything, then?"

"No problem!"

"An independent little soul!" That's what his grand-mother called him these days.

"I've had to be," she said. She'd found a round tea-tray, the mugs, the coffee, the spoons and a packet of biscuits. A half-full bottle of milk, gold top, stood waiting on the counter.

"Sugar?" he said.

"Yes, darling?" She was giggling at him, like a little girl.

"Where's the sugar?" he demanded.

"Don't you know?"

"Yes, of course I know, but you'll never get your Brow-nie badge unless you get it right."

"I don't take sugar," she said.

"I do."

"It's bad for you."

"That's not the point."

"I'm not giving you sugar."

"Everything that's nice is bad for you."

"I bet you've already eaten all those sweets you bought this morning." He hadn't. He'd forgotten about them. They were still jammed in Dad's jacket pocket.

"Well, that's where you're wrong. I resisted them."

"Haven't you done any work at all this afternoon?"

"Yes, I have."

"How much?"

"What is this, the Spanish Inquisition?"

"How much?"

"Plenty."

"Honestly?"

"Honestly. Do you want me to show you?"

"So it's alright if I stay?"

"It's alright," he said.

She was pouring water into the mugs. Simon passed her the sugar bowl and then leaned on the worktop to watch her. She put one spoonful of sugar into one of the mugs.

"OK now?" she asked.

"Two sugars," he said.

"No way!"

He grabbed her wrist and tried to force her to put the second one in.

"Don't you dare!" she snapped. He let go quickly, scared he'd spoilt it, but she smiled up at him. "Try cutting down, starting tonight."

"Why should I?"

"Because I'm asking you to." She looked at him quizzically. He felt himself teetering on the top of a fence. Whichever side he came down on it would be decisive. She was a right little madam, this one.

"Fair enough," he said. He took the tray from her and led the way back into the lounge. She pattered behind him, chattering.

"Gran says, would you mind walking me home because it'll be dark and she'll be worried otherwise."

"I can probably manage that."

"She seems to think I'll be safe with you." Was she teasing him, issuing a challenge? Did he want to be thought safe?

"She's very trusting. Am I going to be safe with you? I'm the baby in this outfit. You're older than me."

"What's age got to do with anything?"

That's what he wanted to hear. He couldn't help the smile which suddenly cracked his face wide open. He felt like a toothpaste advertisement but his mouth didn't seem to want to close. "Anyway," she continued, "you seem older than sixteen." He wondered whether to tell her that he wouldn't even be sixteen until next Tuesday. "How old are you, exactly?"

"I thought age didn't matter?"

"It doesn't."

"Fifteen point nine recurring."

"What?"

"I'll be sixteen a week tomorrow." She didn't answer

and Simon tried to imagine what she was thinking. "Where do you want to sit?" She had a choice of two armchairs, a settee, two stools or a squashy beanbag, so she knelt on the hearthrug and peered at the fire.

"Are you sure you've lit this, Simon?"

"Hang on!" He put the tray down on the floor and then knelt beside her. Somewhere in the bowels of the little mountain he'd built there was a red glow but it was certainly struggling.

"Try that," he said, passing her a short brass poker. He dashed out to get another fire-lighter and the matches but when he got back she'd coaxed tiny orange flames into licking greedily up the sides of the mound.

"The magic touch," he murmured, taking the poker from her and placing it, with a clank, on the hearth.

"Simon," she said softly, "you've just kicked your coffee over." He hesitated a moment, unsure if he was being teased again. "You really have," she insisted. "Mine's the full one."

He really had, but thanks to the raised rim of the tray his coffee was now a perfect circular lake, contained within.

"You can share mine if you like," she offered.

"No sugar," he said, and heaved himself up to start all over again.

The water was still hot so it didn't take long. He dried the bottom of her full mug with a cloth, made himself a fresh cup and left the tray in the sink. He carried the two mugs back, very carefully, and placed them on coasters on the mantelpiece.

"Sorry about the biscuits," he explained. "They're a bit soggy."

"It's OK. I'm trying to diet anyway."

"Good idea!" he said, before he could help himself, then, holding up his hands in mock surrender, "I didn't mean it! Honestly."

She had moved from the rug to the armchair so he passed over her mug, which she cradled on her lap. Every other seat was too far away from her so he opted for the rug for himself, ostensibly to keep a check on the fire. Unwilling to go out again, he used the fire tongs to transfer a few small pieces of coal from the brass scuttle to the fire, placing them delicately in every convenient hollow. The flames changed course, searching and enveloping. He replaced the tongs on their hook, reached up for his coffee and then settled himself, his back against her chair and her knees, his own long legs stretched out. He felt her stir and then a hand touch the back of his hair, briefly.

"Thanks for looking after me this morning," she said. He turned himself round to face her, his arms across her knees.

"If you hadn't come tonight," he admitted, "I'd have been cycling up and down your lane for hours, you know."

"I know."

"Why did you come?" He wanted to make her say how she felt, wanted to hear her say it.

"Because I needed to see you. You just walked away this morning, without a word. I was only going to walk past your house but I saw your dad go out in the car so I thought I'd risk it."

"Risk what?"

"Whatever you might say. You might have told me to get lost. Gran thinks I'm very forward and you're probably just too polite to tell me."

"To tell you what?"

"That I'm a nuisance and that you've got better things to do."

"You're a nuisance." He rested his chin on her knee and looked up at her.

"No I'm not. You've already missed your chance to get rid of me."

"How did you know where I lived?"

"Gran and the phone book."

She was so unlike the girls at school who whispered in groups and shared all their experiences and yet couldn't give a straight and simple reply to a direct question. They would have answered, "Oh, wouldn't you like to know?" or something equally inane. Well if she could be direct, so could he. He placed his coffee cup on the hearth and then took hers from her, placing it out of harm's way. Even as he turned back to her they both heard a car pull into the drive as headlights swept across the front window.

"Visitors?"

"I'm not expecting anyone," he said, scrambling up angrily. He peered through the curtains. "It's my dad," he said. "What's he come back for?"

"Do you want me to go?"

"No. Stay there. He's probably forgotten something vital." Simon went to open the front door, intending to speed his father's departure.

His father was annoyed. Only three people had turned up for the meeting and, as chairman, he'd immediately cancelled it and come home.

"People think clubs run themselves, Si. They've all got good excuses for not doing the work but they always seem to find the time to play when it suits them."

"Can you do that?" Simon asked. "Just cancel a meeting suddenly?"

"Who cares? I've done it." Well I care, Simon thought, but his dad wasn't to know that.

"So you're staying in, then?"

"Yep. Put the kettle on, son. Let's have a..." He suddenly stopped as he saw Charlie, ensconced in his armchair, and the surprising sight of the fire flickering eagerly in the grate. Before Simon could explain they solved it themselves.

"Hello, Mr. Walters," Charlie said, rising confidently. "I'm Charlotte Barber, a friend of Simon's. I hope you don't mind my dropping in like this."

"No, not at all." Simon watched the familiar transformation as his father slipped into his public image. He extended his hand and shook Charlie's warmly. His smile was a more practised version of Simon's. The tension seemed to slide from his face at the sight of her.

"Not at all. It's a pleasure to meet you. Do sit down again. Would you like a drink?"

"No thank you. We've just had coffee."

"I'll get you one, Dad," Simon chipped in. He left them to it but hovered in the hall a moment, listening.

"Have we met before?" his father asked, obviously wondering how Simon had kept him from her.

"No. I don't live in the village. I'm staying here temporarily, with my grandmother. Mrs. Hadley, Holly Cottage. Do you know her?"

"I don't think I do. Simon's mother knew everyone but, working in London, one doesn't become part of village life."

"It sounds like the best of both worlds," she said, flattering him. "What do you do in London, Mr. Walters?" Inevitably Dad launched into a description of his activities in the Department of Education and Science. Simon felt it was safe to go and make the coffee without missing anything new or interesting. He felt proud of Charlie. She certainly knew how to handle his father.

Half an hour later desperation was beginning to set in. He hadn't been able to get a word in edgeways and he'd had to sit, watching the pair of them chattering like old friends. Dad had already elicited a potted history of her father's medical career, a description of her house in Cheshire and an edited version of how she had met his son. He was charming her, attentive and considerate, listening. Simon had once asked his mum why she had married Dad, unable to understand how anyone could. It was during a particularly unpleasant battle over a new bike. He'd found his father totally unreasonable, arrogant and insensitive.

"Your dad could charm the ducks off the pond if he wanted to," she'd said, smiling to herself. Here he was now, doing it to Charlie. There was no way he could ever compete. It was like not being in the room at all. Charlie kept glancing at him but his dad was oblivious. No wonder Suzie was special to him. Suzie was female. And Mum, hadn't she danced to his tune?

We're all parasites, he thought, feeding our egos off each other, eager to please in return for the praise that keeps us going, fuels our progress. Like today. With one phone call Charlie had made him feel he mattered to her so he'd become some super-efficient whizz kid for a whole afternoon. She'd turned up this evening, openly paying him the compliment. "I wanted to see you," she'd said and he'd felt he could walk on water. Dad was the kind of man who could do that to women. I'm the kind of man that women can do it to, he thought bitterly.

It was nearly nine o'clock before she attempted to extricate herself. She suggested she ought to be getting back to her grandmother.

"I'll get our coats," Simon said quickly.

"Can I run you home?" his father offered, reaching for his car keys. "It's no trouble."

"Thank you but there's no need," she said firmly. "It's only a few minutes' walk."

"It's cold and it's dark," he insisted. "Come on."

"No, really, Mr. Walters. I'd much rather walk home, with Simon if you don't mind."

Simon had already come in with his ski jacket on. He caught sight of himself in the mirror, approving of the broad-shouldered macho shape it gave him. At least his dad seemed to know when he was beaten and was helping Charlie on with her coat.

"Here," said Simon, offering her a bulky scarf. "It's going to be cold."

"I've offered her a lift," Dad said.

"Yes, I heard you."

Charlie stepped in, holding out her hand to his father. "It's been nice meeting you," she said. "Good luck with your report."

"It'll get finished eventually," he said. "Goodnight. Take care of her, Simon."

Chapter
EIGHT

They stepped out into the darkness. The air was so cold it seemed to cut into their faces. Simon thrust his hands into the high pockets in the jacket and bent forward against the wind.

"Come on," he said. "It's freezing."

She stood still.

"What's the matter?" he asked. She still didn't move. He went back for her, held out his hand and she grabbed it happily.

"How come you always get your own way?" he said.

He'd planned to walk her along the bridle path to Brook Lane. It would be dark and quiet and private, but she wanted to stay on the normal roads to protect her fancy boots. He found himself following the street lamps all the way through the village, in open view. He suddenly realised she was almost trotting at his side. He'd been striding out again.

"Shall I slow down?"

"Please!" she said.

They walked a little further, both of them listening to the sounds of the village settling. A car engine stopped, a door slammed and then a garage door clanged shut. Somewhere down a side-road guests were leaving. A shrill chorus of "Byee! Byeeee!" echoed and then another door slammed. Just as they were passing one house its porch light went off, leaving them in semi-darkness. He considered pulling her to him, into the porch, until a car appeared around the bend and lit them up with its main beam headlamps. When the car had gone they moved on, but ever more slowly.

"Your dad's nice," she said.

"You think so?"

"He treats you like an equal."

"He treats *you* like an equal, you mean."

"Is that why you're cross?"

"Who says I'm cross?"

She didn't pursue it which made him feel even more foolish. He'd given her the kind of answer he might have got from one of the kids at school. He didn't know how to make it right again.

"It's just that I didn't expect him to come home and then he just took over."

"And you felt left out?"

"He always makes me feel left out. He's only interested in making an impression."

"At least he's interested in your friends."

"See, he's already got you on his side."

"Do there have to be sides?"

Did there have to be? It wasn't a contest and even if it had been Simon had clearly won. She was here with him instead of being driven comfortably home. What's more, he was behaving childishly.

"I just wish he wouldn't be two people. He really turns it on in public, especially where women are concerned, and yet he's a miserable old devil most of the time at home."

"Perhaps he feels he doesn't need to put on an act for you. I'd take that as a compliment if I were you."

"What's your old man like?"

"He's just miserable all the time. He's very dedicated and he works very hard so everyone else is expected to make allowances."

"You didn't tell me he was a doctor."

"You didn't ask."

"And you didn't tell me your name was Barber either. I thought it was Charlotte Hadley."

"Gran is my mother's mother. My father's name is Barber."

"The demon Barber!"

"He can be."

Simon squeezed her hand. Maybe he wasn't the only one who had a lot to put up with. "We're nearly there," he said. "Will I see you tomorrow?"

"Twelve o'clock for lunch, providing you've spent the whole morning working."

"You won't know whether I have or I haven't," he taunted.

"No, but you will. It's between you and your conscience. And anyway," she added, "how can we end up at the same university if you fail your exams?"

"You'll have forgotten me long before then," he said.

"You think so?"

"I hope not, but I think so."

"Don't you believe in Fate?"

"You mean destiny, the kind of fate that is meant to be?"

"Yes. Don't you believe that people can be fated to meet?"

"No, I don't think so."

"So it was purely accidental, you and I meeting?"

"Absolutely. If it wasn't an accident Robbie and that Golden Retriever would have to be part of the plot."

"Would you have ended it there if I hadn't waited outside the shop for you?"

"Yes, I expect so."

"So I'm nothing special."

"I didn't say that. I didn't know you then."

She was quiet as they covered the last few yards to the gate. She went to open it by lifting the iron latch off the post but he stopped her. "Don't disappear behind that gate again like you did this morning."

She turned to face him. Simon could feel his pulse beating in his temples and his heartbeat seemed audible in the darkness.

"I didn't say you weren't special," he whispered.

This would be a good moment for her to wrap her arms around his neck, to pull him close, but she didn't. She simply stood there, waiting. If he made the wrong move, if he was clumsy, he'd never forgive himself. He wondered what she was expecting. How experienced was she? Was she playing games with him because the holiday was boring? Would she slap his face if he went too far?

In the end fate intervened. His legs felt suddenly so weak he pulled her to him almost instinctively to help him to stay on his feet. She was so tiny he had to bend down to rest his face on her hair. Her arms went around him tightly and they stood there, just hugging each other. Their breath, visible in the cold, mingled and spiralled upwards, then she wriggled a little to loosen his grasp, pushed her hands up to the front of his collar and gently unzipped his bulky jacket. He held it open while she snuggled in, her arms around him again but this time without the jacket's padding to keep them apart.

"See," he murmured. "You've been getting your own way all day."

She turned her face up to him and he smoothed aside a stray curl with his right hand, still holding her close in the crook of his left arm. Then, hooking his fingers gently into the back of her hair he turned her head until he could kiss her, very gently, very softly, on her eyes, her nose, her cheeks and finally her mouth. He was doing what Kev had once told him.

"Make 'em wait, old son. Take your time. Keep it gentle till they're crying out for it."

It seemed crude to apply Kev's practised technique to Charlie but he didn't dare move too fast and anyway, it seemed to be working. Each time he kissed her a little longer, a little more firmly until finally they were locked together, her arms around his neck forcing his head down. When he came up for air he was breathing heavily and realised that he had been crushing her against the gatepost, probably hurting her.

"Are you OK?"

"Yes," she said. "Are you?"

"I wish we were at home," he said. "I bet there's a lovely fire by now." He knew they were both imagining what might have been.

"You'd better go home now, or I might not let you go at all," she threatened.

"Suits me," he said, kissing her face again but knowing that a furtive grope by the gatepost was not the way they wanted it to be. He opened the gate for her then quietly fastened it again. She leaned over it towards him.

"Do I get a goodnight kiss?"

"What?" he said. "Another one?"

"Just one then I'll go in."

"Come on," he wheedled. "Be honest. I'm just a toy boy, aren't I?"

"All six feet of you," she exclaimed. "Some toy!"

He put his head forward, pursed his lips and closed his eyes. Nothing happened. When he opened them she kissed her fingers then touched his lips with them before scampering off down the path. "Don't forget," she called. "Twelve o'clock tomorrow."

He was home before he knew it. He had half-walked half-run, just for the hell of it. Now all he wanted was the privacy of his own room and bed. He hung his coat up and was half-way up the stairs when his dad emerged from the lounge.

"OK, Simon?"

"Yeah, fine."

"Did you see her home safely?"

"Yes, of course."

Dad was looking at him strangely. "What's the matter? You look a bit flushed," he said with a grin.

"So would you if you'd run all the way home."

"Ah! Is that what you've been doing?"

"Yes. What d'you think I've been doing?"

"She's alright then?"

"Probably fast asleep by now."

"She's a nice girl, I thought. Very grown-up."

He means she's not what he expected me to bring home, Simon thought. He still thinks of me as a child.

"Most of us are these days, Dad, or hadn't you noticed?" Simon continued to climb the stairs.

"Do you not want a drink then?"

"No thanks."

Within five minutes he was in bed, his door closed to the world, his curtains open to the sky. Somewhere across the fields, in a room under the eaves of Holly Cottage, she too would be lying under those same stars. Was she fast asleep or lying, like him, thinking about this most extraordinary day? Last night in bed, this morning in bed, he hadn't even known of her existence. Now he'd give anything to have her with him.

"Goodnight, Charlie Barber," he whispered. "See you tomorrow."

Chapter
NINE

He awoke to the most glorious of October mornings. The sun, slanting through the glass, bathed his head and shoulders in a summer warmth and his window was a square of blue water-colour. He was wide awake, wondering whether to leap out of bed and get the day underway when he decided to run it all through his head just one more time. If he concentrated hard he could still feel her arms tight around him and her head, a warm pressure against his chest, all safe and secure inside the protection of his jacket. If he got up now he'd remember last night but maybe lose the sensation. He wanted to hold it close a little longer.

He'd imagined at first that he was alone but the gentle thud of a cupboard door and the chink of crockery below him meant that his father was still at home. Simon tugged his pillow out from under the covers and put it back under his head. It was warm, comforting. He turned sideways. The clock said seven-fifteen. He'd set the alarm for eight o'clock each day, intending to start work early. Yesterday he'd switched it off almost as soon as it rang, cross with it for bringing him face to face with his obligations. Today he switched it off with a complacent flick of a finger before it could even begin. He remembered feeling the same anticipation on birthday mornings or Christmas Days when, even as a small child, he'd trained himself to lie still just a little longer and a little longer, savouring the prospect of the day ahead, imagining how he'd react.

"Thanks, Mum. Thanks Dad. It's great! Just what I wanted." Usually it was. Except for last Christmas. He'd been so sure it would be the leather jacket his mum had allowed him to try on a fortnight before. She had asked him questions. "Are you sure it's comfortable? Is it roomy enough under the arms? Is it what you really want? It's very expensive, Simon! Let me think about it."

"But Mum, it'll be gone. There's only this one I like." She'd argued. He'd argued. Eventually she'd walked off, ashamed of his petulance, but he knew she'd probably pop back later. He'd lain there, where he was now, on Christmas morning, wondering what to put on to show it off best. He'd opened about half his packages before it dawned on him that it wasn't there. It was when he found the watch.

"Thanks, Mum. Thanks, Dad," he'd said.

"Look after it, Simon. It's a good one," Dad had boasted. Later in the day she'd spoken to him quietly in the kitchen.

"That jacket, Si. Your dad thought it was too expensive for something you'll have grown out of in a year. Best to leave it till you're a bit older." When he hadn't answered she had said, "He's quite right, you know, and you needed a reliable watch for school."

"Yeah. Sure," he'd agreed. "It's really nice." But she'd known how he felt.

That, more than anything, was what he'd lost, that constant and absolute certainty that she'd understand. No words. No explanations. Just that instinctive knowledge. Suzie had done her best for him he knew, shielding him, coaxing him, but he'd lost her already to some thick-set Northerner called Bruce who called her Petal and slapped her bottom at every opportunity. But then, yesterday, in his moment of wretchedness, Charlie had known. In the time it took to walk home she'd realised, spoken to her gran and fixed it. "Can you come for lunch?" she'd said. "Go and have a hot bath," she'd said. And later on, while he was trying to resist the urge to hover outside Holly Cottage, she'd had no such qualms. She was there on his doorstep because that's where she wanted to be. And today he was going for lunch.

He heard the soft click of the front door as Dad tried not to wake him and then the familiar rumble of the car as it headed off for the station. With the house to himself he felt free to emerge so he was already out of the shower and into the Sugar Puffs when she phoned.

"Good morning," she said.

"Good morning. How are you?"

"Very well," she purred down the line. "And how are you?"

"Exceedingly fit."

"Sleep well?"

"Most of the time."

"Are you working?"

"'Struth! It's only eight o'clock."

"You've only got three and a half hours. Don't forget you're coming for lunch."

"Is that likely, woman?"

"What are you going to do this morning?"

"Probably English."

He'd have to start the essays soon. It was now going to be a real struggle to do even enough to keep Davies quiet, especially as he had only four days before Charlie would have to go.

"What's it about?"

"Which one?"

"That bad!"

"That bad," he admitted.

"See you later, then."

"See you later."

He waited for her to replace the receiver, which she did

rather more promptly than he expected. She didn't mess about, that girl.

Not having read enough to start on the literature essay, he decided to do one of the 'expressive' ones first and to be quite calculating about it. Five hundred words equals one and a half to two sides of A4 paper equals about six paragraphs or so. Piece of cake! He'd got some notes somewhere he'd done in a lesson. They took some finding but eventually he found them at the back of his History book which he often used for rough work, tearing out the pages before handing it in. His book looked painfully thin but Lealman never commented anyway.

By ten o'clock it was done. It wasn't brilliant or even especially neat but it was done, a first and last draft. It needed checking but he'd do that later. It was coffee-break time. By half-past eleven he'd almost finished the second. He'd done about four hundred words of a descriptive piece, about racehorses training up on the gallops, when the phone rang again.

"I haven't forgotten," he said.

"What?" said Kev. "It's me."

"'Allo, mate. Thought you were in Ireland."

"I was but I'm back. Who did you think I was?"

"Oh – someone else. What ya doing back anyway? You said you'd be away all week."

"It's a long story," said Kev. "Can I come round?"

"Yeah, sure." Kev sounded strange. "When d'you want to come?"

"I'll come now." Simon looked at his watch.

"Could you make it later only...well it's a long story too but I've got to see someone for lunch." There was a pause.

"Two o'clock?" Damn, thought Simon. Charlie would be expecting him to be free. He wanted to be free. "I don't have to come," Kev said, filling in the silence, but something sounded unlike Kevin.

"No. Two o'clock's fine. I'll get back," Simon said, remembering how Kev had always been there when he needed him. "Are you alright?"

"Tired. We've been travelling half the night."

"What's happened?"

"Can't explain now. I'll see you later."

"OK. See ya!"

It wasn't like Kevin to play guessing games. Simon had never heard him sound so deflated and odd. By the time he set out for Holly Cottage he felt totally mystified and restless and yet he didn't want two o'clock to come because that would mean his lunch-date was over already.

The day glittered all around him. Every blade of grass shone wetly. Even the gravel in next door's drive seemed to have been scattered with tiny jewels. Mrs. Green had a tall yew hedge which, like a dark, swelling wall, shadowed him for a moment or two, but above that a stunning tree with rich, red, feathery leaves glowed like a torch. Further down the hill the Jacksons' hawthorn hedge glinted, a green-gold tweed, parts of it still deep, glossy green but much of it already yellowing unevenly. "Season of mists?" he said to himself. "No way!" He almost went home for his sunglasses. His foot squelched into a rotten apple that had fallen onto the pavement from old Mr. Simpson's Bramley. He walked over to the verge, to clean his shoe on the grass. The council had been recently to mow it. Like a shimmering green rug it winked up at him, stirring memories he didn't want, not today. He stamped crossly and hurried on.

He stayed on the south side of the main street, away from the bustle in front of the shops. Maureen was outside, cleaning one of the big windows with a squeezy mop on a long handle. He didn't call to her and then felt guilty. A friendly wave wouldn't have been too much trouble. The girl with the push-chair was there too, gazing into the cake shop window, deliberately ignoring Wayne who was tugging at her skirt. He tried to imagine Charlie like that then banished the vision. No one in his right mind would force her into that. Charlie's kids wouldn't have runny noses or straggly hair or be pushed around in tatty plastic push-chairs. He had a fleeting glimpse of responsibility, of the need to provide.

The cottage gate was warm to the touch. The wood was old, the paint flaky, but he liked the squeak as it swung open, perfectly balanced on great metal hinges. Shutting it was harder. The drive sloped downwards so he had to push the great weight of the gate uphill and hold it while he hooked the catch over the gatepost. He wondered how Charlie or her grandmother managed it. By the time he turned round she was there, at the door, looking like a child again in striped Andy Pandy dungarees.

"So how much have you done?" she asked.

"Plenty," he said, grinning. "I'm firing on all cylinders."

"Lucky us! Come on in. It's nearly ready."

She led him through a tiny square porch full of plants into a living room. It was much darker inside and his eyes took time to adjust but, bit by bit, he began to discover the room. A coal fire burned behind the glass doors of a stove and it was very warm. He was glad to hand Charlie his jacket. A small window looked out onto a pretty, well-tended garden at the back where Robbie lay in the sun and, in front of the window, a table was set for three. The cloth was white and in the centre, in a tiny white vase, Charlie had put the head of a blue hydrangea, one of the few not yet faded.

"Smells good," he said.

"Have a seat while I hang this up," she said. "I'll tell Gran you're here."

Gran was much smaller than he remembered but otherwise much the same. Her hair, white rather than grey, was neatly styled and she stood very upright. She wore smart shoes with heels and a swinging pleated skirt. The apron she was wearing for protection was pretty and frilly. She's the antithesis of batty Nora, he thought.

"Simon, my dear," she exclaimed, as if he'd weeded her garden only yesterday. "How nice to see you again."

"Thanks for inviting me," he said.

"It's our pleasure. We get lazy, Charlotte and I, living on little snacks, don't we? It's nice to have a man to cook for."

He felt rather foolish. She was patronising him, being nice to Charlotte's little friend, but then he felt annoyed with himself as she added, "It's nine years since Mr. Hadley went. There's no fun in cooking for yourself."

"I made the pudding," Charlie announced, "so you'd better say you like it."

"I'm sure I shall."

"He'll say so even if it's awful, which it isn't," Gran added.

They sat at the table, the three of them, over the best meal he'd had for months, home-made meat pie, apple crumble with cream and fancy cheese. Even the coffee was freshly ground. They discussed school and university, their prospects and their hopes. Mrs. Hadley told them shocking little stories of her own schoolgirl pranks, making them laugh, testing their credulity. They'd had gas mantles, not electric light, and open fires with huge iron fire-guards, and inkwells with dip-in pens. The toilets were in a separate block at the end of the school-yard, non-flushing and stinking. Each night the caretaker would fill buckets of water from an outside tap to flush them for the next day.

"I hardly ever used them," she said. "I'd rather have wet my knickers than go in there. I used to run home, bursting, and my mum used to have all the doors open ready." She paused then went on, "But what I hated most of all was snow. There was this big lad, Reg his name was, who lived near us. He always used to pull my plaits or squirt me with water but when it snowed, he'd pelt me with snowballs till he made me cry. I can still feel the sting of them. My face would go all red and purple and if there were no teachers or big girls around he used to stuff snow down my back. Once I struggled so hard he got really mad. I kicked him as hard as I could so he pushed me over and crushed my face into the snow. It was all dirty and slushy where we'd been trampling about and then he told me he'd seen the caretaker's dog piddling just there earlier on. I ran out of school and all the way home. My mother dried me, changed my clothes then took me back again. Reg got the cane that time."

"What a lout!" said Charlie. "How did he turn out in the end?"

"We were married for twenty-eight years," she said.

"But Grandad's name wasn't Reg!" Charlie complained.

"It was, but I hated it and so did he so I called him Jim. His middle name was James."

"How come you married a lout?"

"He grew out of it. Boys tend to improve as they get older."

"I know," Charlie said.

Mrs. Hadley began to clear the table. Simon offered to help.

"I wouldn't dream of it, Simon. It will all go in the dishwasher."

Charlie began to carry things out too and he was left to his own devices. On the wall above the fireplace there were lots of tiny brass-framed pictures, mostly family photographs. He found several that were obviously Charlie at different stages: a little toddler in a short, flouncy dress with a huge ribbon in her hair and a rag doll trailing from one hand; Charlie as a bridesmaid with a coronet of flowers and a long dress, and a much more recent one, Charlie next to a tall, impressive-looking man who had an arm around her shoulders.

"Is this your father?" he asked as she trotted in for more dishes.

"No," she said. "That's Uncle John. He came over, about eighteen months ago. He lives in Canada."

"Whereabouts in Canada?"

"Toronto, or very near Toronto. Gran will know exactly, if you ask her."

"My sister's meeting people from Canada this week," he told her. "Relatives of her boyfriend, Bruce."

"Bruce," she said. "Sounds like a lumberjack."

"Looks like one too."

"Don't you like him?"

"He's ok."

"How old's your sister?" she called, trundling towards the kitchen again.

"Nineteen."

"What's her name?"

"Suzie. Suzanne."

She came back in, carrying their coats. "Where's Suzie this week then?"

"Up in the Lake District, staying with Bruce's family. I expect she's enjoying herself."

"Sheltering from the rain more likely. I've never been to the Lake District when it wasn't raining."

"I've never been at all," Simon said ruefully.

"Well, there's something to look forward to," she teased. "Now, we're going to Newbury for a look around the shops this afternoon. Gran says you can come if you like but I'll understand if you've got to work."

"I've got to work."

"OK. But I'll be back by tea-time."

"Right."

Simon put his jacket on, zipping it up slowly, avoiding her eyes.

"Thanks, Mrs. Hadley," he shouted. "I'm off now."

"Bye, Simon dear. Don't work too hard."

"No chance, don't worry." He finally looked at her.

"Have a good time in Newbury," he said. She let him get as far as the door before she spoke.

"Simon!"

"Yeah?"

"Shall I see you later?"

"Yeah," he said and kissed the top of her head.

He should have told her about Kev but he didn't really know what he could have said. He'd explain later, when he'd heard the long story.

Kevin arrived at two minutes to two. He looked pale, dishevelled, in need of a shave.

"Come in," Simon muttered, alarmed by this unlikely version of his friend. "When did you get back?"

"This morning. Just before I rang you."

"Did something go wrong?"

"You could say that!" Kevin spat out the words.

"You look awful."

"Thanks."

"No, I mean tired, not yourself."

"It's a long story."

"So you said."

They sat in the conservatory, hugging two cans of beer, while Kevin did his best to explain. They'd set out to visit his Aunty Pat who lived in Dublin. They hadn't seen her for years but she'd written, out of the blue, to suggest that Kev's mum should go over, with the three kids, for a break. By working overtime his mother had scraped together their fares and Kevin had contributed too. He'd worked on a farm all summer and had saved a fair bit. When they arrived they'd been made very welcome, though the sleeping arrangements were a bit cramped. His sisters had air-beds on the floor of his mother's bedroom. Kevin had slept on the settee downstairs.

His Aunty Pat fussed a lot and did very little. They were quite hungry much of the time but it wasn't too awful until Monday lunch-time when Kevin had heard his mum and Pat yelling at each other like children. He'd run upstairs to find his mother sobbing and Pat waving a coarse finger at her.

"There's many a good Irish girl that'd be glad of a man like our Michael, who'd not drive him from his own home with her naggin' and wailin'."

They'd been set up. Kevin's dad had turned up in Dublin a few weeks earlier and persuaded Pat to invite his family over.

"A man's entitled to see his own kids," she'd said, "whatever he's supposed to have done."

"He was there, Si, in a boarding-house round the corner, just waiting and watching. Pat said he'd watched us arrive. Now he wanted to talk to us, to explain, she said. Three years without even a postcard and then there he was."

"And your mum was upset."

"You could say that. Within fifteen minutes she'd got us all packed and ready. No way was she going to speak to him, she said, so Pat said that was alright as it was us kids he wanted to see anyway. Rosie was crying by then, scared of seeing him again, and Mary sided with Mum and called him a selfish bastard and a few worse things, so then Pat started laying into my mum and it was awful." He stopped for a while, remembering. "Then Pat went out, to get him I think, and Mum made me phone for a taxi. It all happened so quickly. One minute we were there, scared he'd walk in, and the next minute we were speeding away in this old banger behind some Irish goblin with no teeth."

"No teeth!"

"Just gums, Si. Wrinkled, red gums. He kept grinning at us in the driving mirror."

Kevin sat very still, more still than Simon had ever seen him. Simon took a few sips of the beer, disliking the taste but appreciating the frothy coldness of it. Eventually he ventured to ask.

"So, in the end, you didn't get to meet up again after all?"

Slowly Kevin shook his head. "But he was there, Si, so close. Just round the bloody corner." He looked straight across the table. "Just round the bloody corner," he said and the tears spilled silently down.

"What I don't understand," Charlie said, "is why he didn't say how he felt. Surely his mum would have let him talk to his dad even if she didn't want to see him." They were sitting close together in the corner of the public bar of The White Lion, as far from the light and the door as they could get. Simon had chosen this pub because it was tiny, scruffy and unfashionable and, tucked away at the edge of the village, less likely to be frequented by neighbours or friends of his father. The locals used The Roebuck, centrally located and newly decorated. It served Real Ale, salad and quiche. The White Lion had wooden benches, chipped glasses and an abundance of elderly customers who traded racing tips and gardening hints, but it seemed safer. With two half-pints of shandy and several packets of crisps they were content to be ignored.

"It's not a very romantic place," he had warned her, "but it will be warm I should think." They had wandered the lanes for a while but the golden day had faded, the night was cold and the damp seemed to seep into their clothes. In either house they would have been forced to make polite conversation. "That's the trouble with country life," he explained. "There's absolutely nowhere to go."

He had hoped to be cool about it but it wasn't easy. He tried to prepare himself for the worst, for the possible humiliation of being turned away. In his head he practised a dignified response. "That's probably just as well. Not our sort of place anyway!" but he was praying it wouldn't happen. As they reached the doorway he'd clasped Charlie's hand a little tighter.

"It'll be alright," she had whispered. "You would pass for eighteen any day."

She'd been quite right. The landlord, a big-bellied, heavy-jowled figure in a grubby sweater, had trundled over without even looking at him properly, too engrossed in another conversation to care whom he was serving. A weathered little man, all tweedy and leathery, was perched like a gnome on a barstool, elbows in the slops, and his little mouth was working like bellows, huffing out the words. He'd been hauled over the coals by his employer, it seemed, and, in language that Simon hoped Charlie couldn't hear, he was telling his bitter tale. The landlord fuelled his anger with timely support: "Aye!" "Right." "I should say so." "You wanna tell 'im." The youngsters had been able to slip comfortably into their corner unchallenged.

Telling her about Kevin had just happened. He didn't normally spread private details around but he needed someone to share it with.

"I've never seen him like that before," Simon explained. "He never seems to have problems like the rest of us."

"Not even when his dad left?" Charlie asked.

"He just seemed to take it in his stride at the time." It was hard to believe now that Kevin hadn't been affected in any way and Simon withered a little at the thought that he hadn't noticed or cared at all. "I didn't really know him so well then," he muttered.

He'd found himself explaining why Kevin had come back with his mum and sisters, left his father behind in Ireland, throwing away the chance of seeing him, of hearing his explanations, without so much as a protest. "His mum is ever so nice but she gets very emotional. She'd have been in hysterics and Kevin's always trying to look after her, to keep her going. I don't think he really thought about it till it was too late."

"What's he going to do now?"

"Don't know. He could write to his auntie. That's what I suggested but he wasn't too keen on the idea." They sat quietly for a while, pondering.

"If you've got family you shouldn't let them slip away," Charlie suddenly said and Simon's mind opened like a vault. Memories he'd once rolled a stone across now tumbled forth.

A pale coffin slipped away into the earth through a narrow door that had been closing even before they left the grounds. He'd turned at the lich-gate just once. Two determined workmen were already shovelling dirt back into the pit. He'd gone to school one morning, hurried and thoughtless, and while he'd laughed in the changing-rooms, chatted over lunch and laboured through the lessons she'd slipped away. While hundreds of schoolchildren sang, like trained parrots, of a crucified Lord who 'died to save us all' she had died alone, needlessly, for no purpose whatsoever.

"He'll probably regret it one day."

"What?" Her voice brought him back.

"Kevin. He'll regret it one day."

"Regret what?"

"Leaving without seeing his father again." Simon thought he had already explained it clearly.

"He already regrets it. That's what he was so upset about."

Suddenly Simon wasn't sure. Kevin had said the worst part was hearing the awful things Auntie Pat had called his mum. He'd been so angry at the time all he wanted to do was to get everyone out of there. It was only on the long journey home that he'd begun to recognise the grains of truth behind the accusations, begun to see for the first time in three years, for the first time in his life, that there might be two sides to the story. All that time he had been hating his dad for abandoning them without ever considering that his dad might be hating it too. Kevin had used Simon as a sounding board.

"I kept thinking of him in that boarding-house, waiting, hoping, all on his own. And watching us, Si. He'd been hiding somewhere, watching us arrive." Kev had paused and Simon had remained silent, afraid to comment. "I might still have hated him if I'd talked to him, mightn't I? But supposing he's changed? What if it wasn't all his fault? What if something happened and he had to go away? Mum never explained anything. She just kept telling us he was useless and we were better off on our own."

Simon had a mental picture of Auntie Pat as a skinny, angular creature, chain-smoking, hard-drinking, lazy, with a voice like a fog-horn and a venomous streak, like a cartoon witch sent to corrupt Kevin's thinking. Then she became a large, homely woman, slovenly but kind, driven to lose her temper by this ungrateful visitor who refused even to contemplate the reconciliation she'd dreamed of and put herself out to create.

"What's your auntie like?" Simon had asked.

"Irish!" he'd said.

What was Kevin so upset about? Not meeting his father or being forced to look at things differently?

"I think," he said to Charlie eventually, "he's discovering that life isn't simple."

"It happens to everyone sooner or later, doesn't it? We all find out that our parents are just ordinary people and not perfect. It's easier to accept your own limitations than to face home truths about your family." Charlie obviously had something on her mind.

"Sounds like it has happened to you," Simon said, prompting her.

"My dad's a clever man, or so people tell me, but there's a part of him missing. Whatever it is that makes people vulnerable and understanding – human rather than a machine – my dad's lost that."

"But he's a doctor isn't he?"

"He's a surgeon," Charlie corrected. "Because he knows how to take people apart and put them back together again he seems to think that's all there is." Simon looked at her to see if she were being flippant but her face was solemn for once, deadly serious.

"I can't believe that," he said. "You said yourself he's intelligent. How can any doctor, surgeon or any other kind, not care about people?"

"I used to think that," Charlie said. "I used to think it was just me he didn't care about because I was a burden to him, holding him back, or because my mother died soon after I was born and it was my fault." Simon swallowed. "But one day it all fell into place. A medical student, Gareth Somebody-or-other, came to see my father at the house. Dad was out but this chap said he'd wait so I let him in. He was really nice and we talked for ages. He said Dad was a brilliant surgeon but impossible to work for. He's sarcastic to students, demanding to all the young doctors, rude to the nurses and supercilious with patients."

"Is that all?"

"Isn't it enough?"

"Why did he tell you all that, I wonder?"

"Because he'd come to tell Dad."

"You're joking!"

"He'd come to tell Dad as a service to future generations, he said. He'd just heard that he'd passed his final exams and that he could take up a post in a different hospital so he'd decided to tell the old sod what he thought of him."

"And did he?"

"I don't know. Dad phoned to say he'd been held up, some emergency operation they needed him for, and Gareth had to leave. He said it was typical. Just when he'd worked up the courage to score a point for the downtrodden masses..."

"So what happened?"

"Nothing. I didn't tell Dad and if Gareth ever did he certainly didn't mention it to me."

"Gareth?"

"No, Dad."

"What was he like, this young doctor? Would you trust his judgement?"

"Oh yes," she said. "It fitted with what I'd known all along really, but it was awful knowing that nobody liked him. My gran doesn't like him either."

"What, this gran? Mrs. Hadley you mean?"

"Mmm. That's why we hardly ever come here. Dad's too busy and Gran doesn't want to see him anyway, though I think she'd like to see more of me."

"Don't blame her," Simon said but Charlie ignored the well-meaning comment.

"Gareth said he's too cold even to be conceited."

"What does that mean exactly?"

"Some successful people start to believe their own publicity, he said, but my dad doesn't even know how good he is. He's just got a one-track mind and gets on with the job. That's why I said he had a bit missing."

Simon pulled her close to him and put both arms around her, locking her in and Gareth out.

"You don't have to believe everything you're told. Maybe this fellow had been told off and wanted to get his own back." He'd decided he didn't like Gareth. "Have you seen him since?"

"No. He'd hardly want to be friends with the demon's daughter, would he?"

"Did you fancy him?"

"Yes, a bit I suppose." She looked up at him shyly then made a sign with her fingers that meant only a tiny bit. Simon took her hand. "At least he had compassion," she added. "He even apologised for insulting my father and then told me I should be very proud of what he'd achieved."

"And are you?"

"Yes," she said eventually. "I am proud of what he has done, what he can do. He's just single-minded, you see."

"Like a shark?"

"Like anyone who is any good at anything. But if we were all like that the world would be a terrible place."

"It's not fantastic as it is."

"No, I know, but most people care about people's feelings. I do. Gran does. You do."

"Yes," Simon said. "I promise you I haven't got a bit missing," and he kissed her hair lightly.

"Anyway, I was only trying to explain that Kevin isn't the only one who's had to face the truth."

Simon understood how she felt and tried to imagine what it would be like if everyone disliked his father. It would be hard to live down. Everyone thought his dad was 'charming'. He'd enjoyed being called 'a chip off the old block' when he was little, when he'd cracked a joke or kissed the ladies before going off to bed. Everybody respected his mum. He'd never had to listen to anyone calling her cruel names. For the first time in six months he felt gifted, lucky, instead of robbed and resentful. He didn't deserve his family any more than Charlie and Kevin deserved theirs. He leaned sideways and, putting his mouth to her ear, whispered.

"If it's any consolation you're nothing like your father, apart from being a genius of course."

"I'm a bit pushy though, aren't I?"

"In the nicest possible way...yes."

"It's just that I can't bear anyone to be lonely just because they're shy. I used to be like that. I was never encouraged to make friends, didn't know how to really. One day someone called me a snooty, stuck-up little prig. I was so upset I went home and cried but then afterwards realised that's exactly what it looked like to other people."

"I can't even imagine you like that."

"I decided that I'd never be like that again. It was hard at first. You risk rejection every time you make the first move but I kept going. I can be single-minded, too."

"I had noticed!" He couldn't see her face the way she was sitting so he turned her towards him. "How come I got picked for the Charlie Barber treatment?"

"Fate," she said. "Once I realised that I'd enjoyed bumping into you, your fate was sealed. I couldn't walk away and miss an opportunity, could I? Mind you, it wasn't easy. You kept wanting to leave and even after the walk you just went off. I didn't know if you'd want to see me again." Simon grinned happily.

"I was shy," he said.

"You weren't shy last night," she reminded him.

"I got over it!" He leaned forward and kissed her, slipping his hand under her coat and around her waist. He felt her relax and sigh.

"Eh, you two! This may be a public bar but we're not licensed for that sort o' caper." It was the landlord collecting glasses. Simon felt a flush rising but Charlie seemed equal to it as always.

"Sorry," she said. "We promise we'll be good."

"I don't mind a little kiss," he rumbled, "as long as it's me what's doin' it." He leered at Charlie and his huge belly shook with amusement.

"Fancy asking tonight," she taunted him, "when I'm already spoken for." The gnome at the bar joined in.

"'E doesn't mind what night, darlin'," he croaked. The landlord laughed again, a coarse, obscene cackle. Simon knew what he was thinking. He didn't know how to get her out of the situation.

"It's alright, girlie," said the fat man. "I just wish I was in 'is shoes," and he gave Simon an envious wink.

When he had moved away Simon looked at her sternly, like a disappointed father. "How can you flirt with that?" he asked.

"It's the sort of thing he expects. He's in a good mood now. If I'd been a prig again he might have taken a closer look at us, maybe even thrown us out." She sent him off to get more drinks and watched approvingly as the landlord served him and chatted good-naturedly to him across the bar.

"What did he say?" she asked as Simon sat down again.

"Told me to get stuck in but not here," he said.

"How crude!" Simon sipped his drink and watched her watching him. "What did you say?" she demanded. Looking straight at her still he put down his glass and then bent nearer.

"I told him," he murmured, watching her eyes, "that I'd got it all in hand."

"And have you?" Was she teasing him?

"I'll do my best."

"I bet you will too, Simon Walters!"

Further conversation was made impossible, however, by a sudden explosion of sound. There was a crashing chord from a tinny-sounding piano, a cheer from the inmates and then a shout of, "Right, Lil, what's it to be?" The gnome was now seated on a piano-stool which had been wound up to its highest level so that his toes barely touched the pedals.

"*If you were the only*," someone called and a large beaming woman rose from her seat and went to stand by the piano. To the cheerful, lilting accompaniment that flowed from those gnarled little fingers she began to sing.

"*If I were the only girl in the world*
And you were the only boy..."

Everyone in the bar except Simon and Charlie seemed to know it, and they all joined in, swaying contentedly while the woman's music-hall soprano rose above them all. It was like a scene from an East End pub show, the kind they put on the TV near Christmas. Simon had no idea such things could happen so close to home. They grinned at each other, amazed and delighted, part of a happy world.

The second song was an old Gracie Fields number, *The Biggest Aspidistra in the World*. Simon had heard it before. The woman sang it well, making them laugh, holding everyone's attention, and both of them joined in with the chorus, shouting out the title line each time it came round. At the end everybody clapped and whistled.

"Buy 'er another one," a voice cried and a sticky red drink appeared on top of the piano.

The singer took a sip or two and then nodded to the

gnome. As soon as he touched the keys Simon knew what was coming next. He was never sure afterwards whether it had been a premonition or whether he had recognised the chord but he had already leaned back, bracing himself, before she began to sing.

"*Sally! Salleeeeee!*"

He knew every word. He'd grown up with it. His dad had sung it so often he'd known it even before he knew nursery rhymes. Whenever his mum had been cross, Dad had spread his arms wide and sung, "*When skies are blue you're beguiling and when they're grey you're still smiling, smi-i-ling.*" The crosser she got the louder he'd sing until they'd both dissolve into fits of helpless laughter. When he was tiny they'd taught him to sing the lines:

"*Sally, Sally, don't ever wander*
Away from the alley and me."

It had been his party piece.

He glanced at Charlie. She was happy, enjoying every moment, joining in with odd words where she could. It was just another song to her. He rested his head against the wall behind him and closed his eyes, letting the melody wash over him. It was his mother they were singing about, not any old Sally, and the face he'd known for so many years yet never really studied was suddenly there, in his mind, as clear and detailed as if she were standing right in front of him. She was smiling at him, loving him still.

He had tried so hard over the months to conjure this but it had been a blur or the sudden memory of the mask, the bland face of her death. He'd caught her voice now and again in Suzie's chuckle or in his grandmother's phrasing but never this clarity of vision. He kept his eyes closed until the song ended, holding her face in his head, knowing at last that it was there in his mind and it could be resurrected.

As the last note faded and everyone clapped once more, Charlie leaned back against him. "What time is it?" she said. He showed her his watch. "Oh God! It's twenty to eleven. I promised to be back by ten-thirty. Gran worries."

Before the applause had died down they were out of the door and into the darkness. "Come on," Charlie said and raced away from him. He had to run faster than he'd expected to overtake her. He ran twenty yards ahead and slid into the shadow of a gateway. "I know you're there," she called. "Simon?" and then a little less confidently, "Simon?" He allowed her to pass him, intending to jump out on her and frighten her, but she looked so little and frantic, hurrying alone in the empty lane, that he changed his mind. Instead he caught her up.

"It's alright. I'm here." She stopped, grateful as he appeared at her side. "How can I take care of you if you run off?"

"I'm late. Gran will be having kittens."

"OK. We'll run," he said, grabbing her hand, and together they raced back to Holly Cottage. There were no street lights until they reached the main road but their feet flew unobstructed along the hidden tarmac. They crossed the road just as a car rounded the bend to the left of them, its lights illuminating their route, but by the time it reached the spot they were already thirty yards up Brook Lane. Simon pulled her along, forgetting the difference in their stride. They arrived elated and breathless at the gate, Charlie holding her side. Mrs. Hadley was on the step, framed in the light of the open door, peering into the darkness. Robbie saw them first and came yapping up to the gate.

"Sshh," Charlie gasped. "We're here, Gran."

"Sorry, Mrs. Hadley," Simon added. "We've run all the way back."

"At least you're safe. Are you coming in now, Charlotte? It's very late." It was a command.

"See you tomorrow," Charlie said as she hurried in, leaving him to fasten the heavy gate.

"I'll phone early," he promised.

"You'd better," she replied, sure of her ownership now and Simon knew she was smiling in the dark.

He decided to walk home, allowing time for his breathing to settle, savouring the sharpness of the frosty air against his skin. He was still glowing after the run, still hearing the music and laughter they'd just left. "Well, Mum," he asked of the night, "what do you think of it so far?" Nothing answered except his own certainty. She'd have liked Charlotte. She couldn't abide bitchy girls. She'd have recognised the danger signs too. "Yes, I know," he said to himself, feeling like a fish on a hook. Charlie had cast her line and he'd taken the bait. What was the phrase? Hook, line and sinker? Worst of all, he'd consciously allowed himself to be reeled in and he didn't care. "No choices," he thought and suddenly he knew what he would say to Kev.

"You can't make things unhappen. Good or bad, we have to accept what's done. Write to your dad, Kev. Take the chance while you can." He would probably refuse but he'd listen and later perhaps, when it suited him, he'd get round to it.

And tomorrow? Tomorrow he'd tell Charlie Barber that he believed in Fate after all.

Chapter ELEVEN

Simon was snatched from a dream of massed choirs, trilling the story of a fishy on a little dishy when the boat comes in, by the strident clock by his left ear. He rolled over to read the time, pressed the button and relaxed back into the warm trough he'd hollowed out for himself. He had to think hard to discover that it was still only Wednesday. 'Wednesday's child is full of woe,' chanted a voice in his head, dredging up some long-forgotten rhyme, but the sun, still astonishingly powerful so late in the year, was spearing through the chinks in his curtains and promising another glittery day. He rolled out from under the duvet and drew back the curtains, making a mental note that the window could do with a clean, and then he opened the door so that he'd hear the phone if it rang. He'd said he would phone her but she was quite likely to ring him if she got tired of waiting. He could afford to give school work a miss for one day. After all she'd be gone after Friday and he could work non-stop all weekend. If he could borrow a bike for her they could go off exploring. Mrs. Hadley might even throw together a picnic for them.

It seemed like a waste of the morning to crawl back in amongst the bedclothes as he was used to doing during the holidays. He checked the time again but it was still only ten past eight. He'd better have breakfast first and give her time to get up. By half-past he was washed, dressed in his newest jeans and sweatshirt, full of cereal and pacing up and down. He forced himself to tidy the kitchen and wash up the few breakfast dishes. Then he hit on the idea of planning their expedition. If he had several routes worked out she could choose the one that appealed to her most. Somewhere, he knew, there should be an Ordnance Survey map of the area. He'd used it for Geography before he abandoned the subject at the end of the third year.

It took him an increasingly irritated five-minute search of cupboards, drawers and bookshelves to decide that Dad had gone off with the map in his car. The last time they used it had been for some tedious Badminton Club treasure hunt early in the summer. They'd all three gone, Suzie as well, and hated every second. Without Mum it had been no fun and their presence seemed to embarrass people who were seeing them for the first time since their 'sad loss', as the vicar always referred to it. Acquaintances who would once have chatted amiably pretended not to see them or smiled weakly as they hurried past. Friends of Dad made a point of coming to speak to them in a kind of strictly-timed rotation as if they had previously agreed to rescue each other from the ordeal. What is more they hadn't won the prize either. They were pipped at the post by a yuppy couple called Marina and Tom who had joined the club very recently, already won a mixed doubles tournament and were hot favourites for the two singles titles. Simon and Suzie had gone for their father's sake and had not expected to have a thrilling time but Dad had come home very depressed and disappointed.

"We nearly won, Dad. It's only because they had a sports car and drove faster than us." He'd tried to cheer him up but later Suzie explained her theory of the male menopause.

"The Toms and Marinas of this world are the new wave, the next generation. They are on the way up, hooked on success, born to achieve. Dad's had his chances already. They make him feel past it. He wouldn't have minded if anyone else had won." Simon had been only half-convinced but was aware in the following weeks of a reluctance in his father whenever social commitments loomed. He'd been determined not to become a recluse, pursuing his old interests with a disciplined dedication after Mum had died, but over the summer he'd lost interest in the outside world, only slipping into the familiar, charming role for the benefit of strangers. Simon wondered how much he had got away with simply because his father was too jaded to argue.

Even the argument they had had last night had been a more civilised affair than Simon's attitude might have warranted. He had arrived home happy, rapidly apologised for his lateness and prepared to confide his experiences for once. He had wondered how his dad would react when he told him about the song and the feeling that he had that his mum was alright. He also wanted to tell someone about Charlie and Kevin and how their parents were such a problem to them. He hadn't got very far when his father exploded.

"You're standing there telling me you've spent the evening in the pub, and in that place of all places, when you're not sixteen yet. Let that be the first and the last time, d'you hear! What could you be thinking of, taking her there? And what is her grandmother going to think? I don't suppose Charlotte's eighteen either."

Simon had tried to explain that it had been a last resort, that it was cold and there was nowhere else to go, that they'd only drunk shandy and sat quietly in a corner and that the pub was maybe a bit rough but it had been warm and friendly and everyone had sung, all the time getting more and more angry as his father's counter-attacks dispelled his euphoria. Did Simon know that there was a fight there most Saturday nights? No, Simon didn't. Did he know that the police were called in regularly to deal with drunken behaviour? No, he didn't. Had he not heard that a man had been knifed up there recently? Yes, he had, but the man was not a villager, was he, and it was at least four years ago, wasn't it? Were those the kind of people he wanted to expose his girlfriends to? Simon remembered his unease and said nothing.

The bubble had been burst and even when they had both calmed down Simon felt he couldn't go back to the other events of the evening. Sullenly he agreed that he would not resort to the pub again until he was older and, yes, he fully appreciated that being cold did not entitle anyone to break the law by drinking under-age.

"You'll be grown-up soon enough, son. Just remember you're only fifteen."

Simon vowed, at that moment, that if he should ever become a parent he would never use this form of control. At five he'd been 'old enough to know better' but not old enough to play on 'the big boys' slide'. At thirteen he'd been told he was a real teenager with all the responsibilities that go with it, as they plotted which household chores he could take over, but he was 'too young' to go Youth Hostelling with a crowd of friends.

"How old do you have to be to live your own life, Dad?"

"I'll tell you when I get there, kid!"

By five minutes to nine Simon had thought of a few possibilities, even without the map, and decided to phone. A frantic search through the telephone directory proved useless so he used his initiative and phoned Directory Inquiries. "I'm sorry, sir," said the trained sing-song voice. "That number is ex-directory." He'd have to go round.

By the time he'd pumped up the squashy tyres, found his trainers, located his keys and some cash and finally set off on his bike, he was beginning to feel pressurised. He chose the top route: up the hill, along the bridle path and a leisurely run down the lane to the cottage. The track was muddy. It clogged his wheels, splattered his jeans and eventually he managed to spray Mrs. Reid, who was up there exercising her fat dachshund, with filthy water from an unfortunately situated puddle.

"Sorry," he called back over his shoulder, knowing he'd

branded himself as an ill-mannered hooligan for evermore in the Reid household. Rounding the curve at the top he almost ran into Jed and Paul Carter who were walking two huge and glossy Alsatians. This time he had to stop. They would have thought it most odd if he had hurtled past as he wanted to do. The dogs sat obediently as the brothers halted.

"Hello, Si. It's a bit early for you, isn't it?" Paul fingered the ski jacket. "Where d'you get this then? Very nice!"

"Reading," said Simon, "in the July sales." He leaned down to fondle the nearest dog, propping the bike between his legs. The Alsatian gazed up with adoring eyes, pushing his head against Simon's fingers. Then the second dog, sensing an opportunity being missed, decided to muscle in, thrusting his face in front of the other one but, on discovering no tit-bits on offer, he backed away again and rubbed himself around Jed's legs before settling down. "I thought these things were supposed to be dangerous," Simon said.

"Soft as butter, these two, as long as you're with us," Jed explained, "but I wouldn't give much for your chances if you tried to break into our place."

"I'll try to remember that next time I'm planning a burglary." Simon grinned then, remembering his only break-in, changed the subject quickly. "What are their names?"

"Fang One and Fang Two," said Paul.

"No, seriously. What are they called?"

"That depends on what they've done and who is calling them. Dad's got some pretty dreadful names for them at times but they're really called Fritz and Samson."

"They're really something," Simon said enviously. "Not like that sausage dog I nearly ran over up there." Paul and Jed patted their pets proudly in much the same way as cousin Keith had patted his sleek Jaguar. "I'd better be off anyway."

"I don't suppose we can guess where," Jed smirked.

"I doubt it," Simon replied confidently.

"Nothing to do with Ma Hadley's granddaughter then?" Simon's mouth dropped open.

"How did you know?"

"Dad was in the pub last night and, unless he's very much mistaken, so were you. With the girl staying at Holly Cottage he said."

"Naughty, naughty!" chided Paul.

"At such a tender age too. Our dad would go mad if he caught us in there."

"Mine already has," Simon admitted.

"Anyway, off you go, lover boy. Don't keep the lady waiting."

"Be a good boy won't you!"

"Or, if you can't be good, be..."

"I know! I know!" Simon pedalled away quickly, his cheeks burning. It would be all round the village before long, then all round the school. By the time he reached the familiar gateway much of the magic seemed to have drained from the day.

Mrs. Hadley answered the door, Robbie scuttling round her feet. She was surprised to see him so early. He explained how he'd promised to telephone without realising that he couldn't get hold of the number.

"Oh, I see," she said, not offering to supply it. "Well, I'm afraid Charlotte isn't up yet, though it's time she was. We're expecting visitors this morning so she won't be free for some time. I'll tell her you called, Simon. I expect she'll be in touch."

"Thanks," he said, helpless on a wave of shock and disappointment.

"Goodbye, dear," and the door was firmly closed.

He made himself walk slowly and with dignity back to his bicycle, not daring to look up or look back, wanting to run to escape this humiliation of his own making. It simply had not occurred to him that she would not be ready and waiting. He swung the gate into place behind him, locking himself out of the place he wanted most to be. He ran the brief conversation through his head. Had he been rude? Was Mrs. Hadley very cool or was that his imagination? Paul and Jed, as well as his father, had thought his pub escapade inappropriate. Was Mrs. Hadley punishing him for that? Could she know? Supposing she didn't tell Charlie he'd been. Supposing Charlie waited all day for the call he couldn't make while he waited for the contact she didn't know she had to make.

He headed downhill towards the shops to give himself a destination. By the time he'd bought a bag of doughnuts and remounted he knew he was aiming for Kev's house. It wasn't until he found himself thumping the peeling door that he realised that this, too, could be an inconvenient moment. Mrs. Halligan let him in. She looked strained and red-eyed and very thin, wrapped in a soiled towelling dressing-gown and padding around in worn velvet mules.

"If you've got the coffee I've got the cakes," he said, doing a quick count in his head, "and there's an extra one for the one who makes it."

"Bless you," she said, patting his arm. "Put the kettle on. I'll get dressed." She pointed towards the tiny kitchen and Simon was never so grateful for a welcome. "Kevin," she shrieked and Simon winced. He heard her clambering up the narrow stairs, cursing to herself each time she trod on something or had to kick it out of the way. Something came bouncing down the stairs with a clatter but he resisted the urge to go and look. Instead he concentrated on finding the kettle amongst the debris. Almost without thinking he began to tidy up, pushing fish and chip wrappers into the bin, stacking plates and wiping the worktop with the only rag he could find.

"You'll make someone a wonderful wife," Kev said from the doorway. He managed to look scruffy even without clothes. He was wearing boxer shorts and a tousled hair-do.

"Just being useful," Simon said. "You alright?"

"Yeah! What're you doing here in the middle of the night?"

"Bearing gifts. D'you fancy a doughnut?"

"Only if it's got jam."

"That's you all over."

The coffee was ready and the doughnuts arranged on a

hastily rinsed plate by the time Mrs. Halligan and the girls appeared. Rosie climbed up onto Kevin's knee and fed him mouthfuls of cake, scraping up the jam splodges from his chest with her finger. Mary had now wrapped herself in her mother's dressing-gown.

Her mother had changed into tight jeans and a baggy jumper. It seemed strange to see that thin, girlish body topped by a once-pretty but definitely aging face. Simon felt only concern. She wasn't equipped for rearing a family by herself. He understood why Kevin had put her needs first.

"I suppose he's told you," she said, winding thin fingers round the chipped mug. Simon nodded. "It's alright," she added. "I don't mind. He needs somebody sensible to talk to. He doesn't get much in the way of sense out of me these days."

"It's an adult disease," Simon explained, "nonsense; it becomes acute in parents and terminal in teachers. It's not being able to see the wood for the trees."

"My mum used to accuse me of that," she said.

"Mine too," he replied.

He stayed an hour and a half with them. Although Mrs. Halligan went out to do some shopping Rosie never left them alone and Mary, older and slyer, hovered within earshot, pretending clumsily to be busy but always watching, listening. They didn't discuss what Kevin should do, though Simon did ask in a roundabout way.

"You've got your aunt's address, I suppose?"

"Yeah, course."

The subject of Charlie couldn't be broached without a long explanation and what he might have told Kevin he certainly wasn't prepared to disclose to his sisters.

He felt calmer when he left than when he'd arrived but within minutes of getting home and seeing the silent phone the frustration had returned. He'd give her till lunch-time. If she hadn't been in touch by then he'd have to call round again.

Trying to work to fill in the time was a non-starter but he

did try. The three-column list looked impressive with two essays ticked off but all he had done was to conquer the molehills while the mountains still lay before him. Soon the page had an intricate border of intertwined letters in various combinations of C, B, S and W. Then he attempted to set himself up for his History project which consisted, so far, of a few scribbled sheets of notes and a daunting list of references that needed to be looked up in books he hadn't got yet. He'd have to get to the library in Newbury. At twelve-thirty he made himself a cheese and pickle sandwich. At twelve-forty-seven the telephone rang.

"Crikey, that was quick," said his father.

"I was in the hall, just passing through," Simon said, trying to control his breathing.

"What have you been doing this morning?"

"Oh, just a little rape and pillage and a quick pub crawl."

"OK. Truce declared. What have you really been doing? This is the third time I've phoned."

"I've been out. Sorry."

"With Charlotte?"

"No. They've got visitors." It sounded no big deal put like that. "I've been to Kev's."

"What about this afternoon? Any plans?"

"Not yet."

"Well, it occurred to me that if you were in town this afternoon you could meet me from the train and we could have a meal somewhere. Charlie, too, if you like."

"Sounds nice but I don't know if she's free."

"Well, you sort it out. I've got to go. If you're there – fine. If not I'll come home. Bye." And he was gone.

Simon recognised a peace offering when it hit him. He could go on his own if necessary and call into the library first. It also gave him a reason for a second visit to Holly Cottage.

"Sorry to bother you again, Mrs. Hadley, but my father has just phoned..."

Chapter
TWELVE

So it was that Wednesday took an upturn. With his new respect for the powers of Fate, Simon reasoned that if he hadn't gone to the pub he would not have had a confrontation with his father who would not then have telephoned his gesture of appeasement to provide the way out of the deadlock. As Fate would have it the day turned chill and cloudy as the afternoon progressed but they hardly noticed. By nine o'clock all four of them, five if you counted Robbie, were ensconced in the warm comfort of the cottage, at least three of them having dined to excess in one of the Newbury hostelries.

"I'm not allowed in pubs," Simon had said but the smell of the food and the stolen glance at the sweet trolley outweighed the need to score points.

"It's different in a restaurant," Mike Walters had argued, changing his tune with the practised ease of a parent.

"What have you been up to?" Mrs. Hadley enquired, pouring frothy hot chocolate from a coffee pot into delicate china mugs.

"Oh, the usual tedious round of meetings and paperwork," answered Mike.

"I think she was asking us, Dad," Simon murmured.

"What have you all been doing, then? Is that better?"
Simon noted with relief that her tone was as friendly and
light as it had been the previous day. She had not only
allowed Charlie to go out with him but had invited them all
in when they brought her home. His father had accepted
readily, perhaps mellowed by the food and the time to
unwind, and also no doubt motivated by his enjoyment of
Charlie's company. She'd made him laugh with tales of her
school life and her recent weeks of sixth-form routine.
Grouped closely round a small polished table, framed in an
umbrella of soft light from the low-hanging lamp, it was
impossible to feel left out. Simon had let them chatter,
filing away the information that poured forth. She was like
a stream, tumbling over herself, leaping from topic to
topic, delighting in an audience that was at once attentive
and encouraging. His dad had teased her, questioned her,
made her explain her opinions, nodded and agreed and
prompted her, guided the flow with well-honed technique.
At one point Simon had warned her playfully.

"You know that anything you say will be taken down and
used in a D.E.S. discussion paper against you, don't you?"

"And so it should," she retorted. "Who is the education
system for, anyway?" and she had bubbled on, punctuating
her remarks with mouthfuls of raspberry torte.

So Simon had sat, content to listen, as he did now.
Draped across the hearthrug, his back resting against his
father's chair, he had enticed Robbie to him and the little
dog now lay with his head and front paws on Simon's thigh,
allowing himself to be tickled and stroked, occasionally
uttering a little rumble to remind the kneading hand to
keep going. He watched Charlie recounting the day's experiences, grinning back at her whenever she caught his
eye. Flames danced behind the glass of the stove and
glinted on the spoon that Mrs. Hadley had passed to him to
stir his chocolate. He held it up and made faces into it, as
he had done that afternoon in one of the three coffee shops
they had visited. Charlie had been telling him about T.S.

Eliot, quoting bits he'd never heard, something about an evening spread out against the sky, and he'd listened to its lilting cadence, letting her teach him. She noticed him now. He looked up.

"I'm measuring out my life in coffee spoons," he said.

"T.S. Eliot," said Dad.

"How do you know?"

"I didn't get where I am today by reading the *Beano*," he laughed.

"The what?" Charlie said.

"The *Beano*. Don't tell me you've never read the *Beano*!"

"Everybody's read the *Beano*, surely?" chirped Mrs. Hadley. Charlie looked bemused.

"It's a comic," said Simon. "Dennis the Menace."

"Minnie the Minx?"

"The Bash Street Kids?" It clearly meant nothing to her.

"Well, well," said his father. "You've obviously had a deprived childhood, Charlotte." Her face clouded for a moment and then Mrs. Hadley restored the mood.

"Simon, tomorrow we must buy her a *Beano*."

"We must supplement her education," said his dad. "Speaking of which, how's the homework coming along so far?"

They all looked at Simon.

"OK," he said.

"He insisted we went to the library this afternoon," Charlotte added supportively, "only it was closed."

"Why was that?"

"Early closing day," Simon admitted. "I'd forgotten." He'd actually had no idea, not having visited it since the days when his mum had dragged him there reluctantly in school holidays to try to get him to choose reading books. He'd even had trouble remembering where it was but fortunately there were not many side-streets to choose from at the south end of the town. He felt he couldn't admit to Charlie that he never used it and was quite grateful that it was shut. At least he didn't have to expose his ignorance of its procedures. His mother had always collected anything he needed when she went shopping. It was just one more thing he was going to have to learn how to do.

"Are you going to have to go in again?" his father asked.

"Could you take me Saturday morning?"

"Anything to avoid the supermarket!"

"I'll come shopping as well."

Charlie smiled. "Tomorrow," she announced, "Gran's got a coffee morning so I shall come round to help you sort out your work and then I'll cook lunch for us while you're doing it."

"Sounds like a good offer, Si. See if you can get his brain working for once," Dad said, looking at Charlie.

"I'm not thick, Dad."

"So I'm told but you could step up your output a little. This holiday is your last chance to prove yourself, I believe." Simon knew. He didn't need to have it stated in public. He suddenly felt like a naughty child again about to be told that he was old enough to know better.

"You're old enough to know the score. Your teachers won't go on making allowances for ever." Simon looked at the floor. Trust Dad to spoil the evening! Robbie inched himself up onto Simon's legs and settled himself full-length, his bright coal-like eyes gazing upwards, reflecting tiny crimson flames. Simon leaned down to nuzzle his rough head.

"He'll be OK," Charlie said, with more assurance than he felt. "You'll see."

The moment passed but the black cloud of his responsibilities had anchored itself back in position. Her account of their afternoon, escaping from the October winds that whipped up the litter and whistled down the alleyways of the town, became the story of his parole, a limited freedom subject to conditions and promises of good behaviour. The handcuffs were on once more. He wanted to stay there all night, knowing that outside the cottage door the rest of the world lay in wait.

At eleven he saw Mrs. Hadley stifle a yawn and felt they should go but was unwilling to suggest it. However, his father must have noticed, too, because he suddenly remarked on the time, thanked them both for a delightful evening and stood up. Simon pushed Robbie off his knee and hauled himself up. It was all over very quickly. Charlie had fetched their jackets and Mrs. Hadley had been shaken warmly by the hand.

"I'll be round about ten," Charlie said. "Is that alright?"

"It gives him time to clean up in your honour," his father said. "He's very good at housework."

"I know," she quipped. "I've seen his apron."

The night air shocked them both. Mrs. Hadley had already shut the door behind them when they turned up their collars and then thrust their hands into their pockets, two figures in unison, father and son.

"I'll do the gate," Simon said and it was cold to the touch, the metal latch making him wish he'd had his gloves on.

The car didn't want to start. It took a third turn of the key before choking into life. "What's wrong with it?" he asked.

"Getting old like the rest of us." They drove home quickly and in silence, each one preoccupied. Simon watched the clouds scudding across the sky, wave upon wave of darkness flowing in and upwards. A half-moon appeared and disappeared during the two-minute journey.

"Is it waxing or waning, Dad?"

"Pardon?"

"The moon, is it waxing or waning?"

"Pass!"

"I thought an educated man would know these things."

"There are a couple of things I don't know. That's one of them."

"What's the other one?"

"I don't know how you are going to spend the rest of your week with Charlotte, as you obviously intend to, and still get your work done."

"I thought you liked her!"

"I do. She's delightful, and I'm pleased that she likes you, but that's not the point, is it?"

"I'll do it. Honestly."

"Good intentions are one thing, success is another."

"Don't go on."

They were home and Simon was on his way up to bed when his father called him back.

"She's a nice girl, Simon. I hope you treat her with respect."

"Why wouldn't I?"

"You know what I mean." Simon did. "No more pubs, alright?"

"No more pubs."

"And if I go out tomorrow night and you have the house to yourselves for a couple of hours I can trust you, I hope, to be sensible."

"Oh Dad, for heaven's sake!"

"You're growing up, Simon. I just want you to be careful, that's all. Lives get ruined very easily." Simon remembered the girl at the shops, Wayne's mum.

"I know. Is this going to be the birds and the bees?"

"No."

"Because if there's anything you want to know you only have to ask."

"Get off with you. Go to bed, but just remember..."

"Goodnight, father dear."

Simon undressed quickly. Tomorrow could be quite a day! Didn't they know he'd never hurt her?

Chapter
THIRTEEN

He really had done quite a reasonable tidying-up job, especially in the kitchen as she planned to cook, by the time the hotline leapt into action again. Simon grinned to himself as he hurried into the hall. Was she double-checking, making sure he was up? It was too early to be Kevin.

"Good morning, Simon. It's Mrs. Hadley. Is Charlotte with you dear?"

"No. She's coming at ten, isn't she?"

"Have you spoken to her this morning?"

"No," and then with a sudden surge of anxiety, "is there anything wrong?"

"I'm sure there isn't. It's just that she's disappeared. It's not like her to go out without telling me. I was sure she'd be with you."

"Perhaps she's on her way. Shall I ask her to phone you when she gets here?"

"Yes, if you would I'd appreciate it." There was a pause and then she said, "Are you sure you haven't spoken on the phone today?"

"I don't know your number, Mrs. Hadley, and this is the first phone call I've had this morning."

"She must have Robbie with her because I can't find

him either."

"Well, that explains it then. Perhaps he got out and she's trying to find him."

"He wouldn't wander away, my dear, even if all the doors and gates were open. She'd only have to call his name." That was true. Simon remembered how he had appeared like magic when she wanted him, how he had run to her to be put on the lead.

"If she's taken him for a walk she'll be back soon. She wasn't planning to bring him here for the day, was she?"

"I'm sure you're right, Simon. Do ask her to phone if she turns up though, won't you."

Typical grandmother! thought Simon. Charlie had said she was a worrier. If Charlie intended to return Robbie before she came round she was probably almost home at this very moment. He set coffee cups and biscuits on a tray, even found a tray-cloth in a drawer. He did a quick check round and decided to vacuum the hall carpet. There'd just be time. When he had finished he pushed the cleaner back into the cupboard under the stairs without winding up the cable and forced the door shut. It was ten minutes to ten. He went to the front window. It was a grey, blustery day. Everything was on the move; trees swayed, leaves were being torn from their twigs, grass rippled. The only ones brave enough to be out were bent low against the rush that seemed to sweep up the hill. Across the road he saw Nora waddle out of the side door clutching a red plastic basket of washing. She disappeared around the back of the house only to emerge a moment or two later in hot pursuit of a flailing shirt that the wind had whipped from her hands. Only a spiky hedge prevented its flight to freedom. Nora grabbed at it angrily. He didn't hear the rip or her furious outburst but the gestures spoke volumes.

There was no sign of Charlie in either direction and for the first time he felt something of the anxiety that he had sensed in her grandmother. She'd be early rather than late, just as she'd have told Mrs. Hadley where she was going, unless she was up to something, some secret surprise. He decided to go and meet her. At least he could hold her down if the wind got too strong.

The route between the two houses was a simple u-shape. She'd be unlikely to use the top way as he'd not shown her that yet. It was possible, once past Mrs. Green's, to see almost to the bottom of the hill and he was disappointed not to see her trudging towards him. It was difficult to look steadily with the wind driving into his face so he watched the footpath pass beneath him and every ten steps he glanced up, each time expecting that this time she would be there. When he reached the main road and turned the corner it was sure to be alright. She'd be hurrying along, a tiny red-coated figure, and they'd run to meet each other like they do in the commercials. He could see a hundred yards or more before the road curved and although there were people fighting their way to or from the shops there was no one remotely like her.

The increase in his heart-rate was not simply a result of exertion. With an effort of will he fought the rising tide of panic that threatened to swamp him. Think, Simon, think! He raced across the road, narrowly missing a passing car, and along towards the familar row of shops. He could see slightly further from this side of the road but it proved no advantage. He dipped into the newsagent's.

"Hi," said a voice at his side. "We meet again."

"Mo, that girl in a red jacket, the one I knocked over, have you seen her today?"

"No. Should I have done?"

"I just wondered if she'd been in."

"Not as far as I know, but I've been busy in the back. She might have."

"OK. I just wondered."

"Shall I tell her you're looking for her if I see her?" Maureen grinned.

"Yes please." He hurried out again, knowing he hadn't been in there long enough to have missed her passing by.

He was fifty yards from Holly Cottage when he realised that he couldn't let Mrs. Hadley see him. As long as she thought Charlie was on her way to see him, or with him, she wouldn't get too agitated, but if he turned up, frantic and alone, they'd both be scared. He turned round and headed back. Where on earth could she have gone? She'd said herself that she hardly knew the village. Where would she take the dog?

Suddenly he knew. If she'd gone for a quick run with Robbie up on the Downs she could have slipped and sprained an ankle or fallen awkwardly. She could be lying up there in the wet grass, injured and helpless, waiting for him to realise and come to her. He'd been so slow, so stupid. If only he'd stopped to think, instead of pottering around with coffee cups and vacuum cleaners, he could have had her home by now. He sprinted along the lane, past the well, past Cooters', past Kevin's, driven by the certainty of his vision. The narrow track was sludgy and slippery. He jumped puddles, skated awkwardly in the slime, side-stepped and danced his way forward, hardly slowing.

The old railway bridge arched darkly above him. He could hear voices, young children, somewhere over his head. They must be playing on the track, now disused and neglected, where he had played years ago. He remembered the excitement of the first time, being so far from home by himself, and the scary feeling he got from the crumbling buildings. "There's ghosts!" someone had said, probably Jed Carter. "And a tramp that eats chickens raw." He scrambled up the embankment, smearing mud across his precious jacket. There were three toddlers building piles of stones along the edge of the track, presumably in order to push them off onto any passing traveller below. One of them was leaning over at a perilous angle, wriggling much too far forward.

"Hey," said Simon. "You'll fall. Move back." A filthy little face peered up at him. It had to be Wayne. He couldn't be more than three or four. Already it had a look of defiance as if to say, "Make me!" Simon took a step forward and the child scrambled to his feet. "Have you seen a girl, probably wearing a red jacket?" The three stared back impassively, as if he'd been speaking a foreign language. He searched hastily in both directions, seeing the parallel lines of darker grass merge at infinity. She probably wouldn't have come up here anyway. He tried once more. "What about a little white dog? About this big," he said, moulding Robbie's shape in the air. Wayne went back to his stones. The other two watched him with wide eyes. He was about to climb down when the smallest of the three boys pointed up the slope, the way he had taken her on Monday. "Thanks, kid," he said, sighing audibly, and he was scrambling down the bank again in a shower of pebbles and dirt.

Once he'd left the boys behind, the slopes stretched emptily ahead. The horses were long gone, back in their stables by now. Could that be why she'd come? To see the racehorses training? Why hadn't she told her gran? He could see the pale swathe of the pathway winding upwards, deserted still, but if she were lying down the long grass would hide her very effectively. He expected at any moment to see the dog or a flash of red and all the time he was striding further and further upwards. He crossed the rough road where they had turned back before and checked in all four directions before moving on. Supposing he'd already passed her? Were there any moments when he'd failed to look sideways? Surely Robbie would have come to him!

He stopped for a breather, scanning the horizon where the Ridgeway seemed to have been stitched like old ribbon along the crest of the hill. The Downs rolled east and west, great swells of land along which Ancient Britons had journeyed in a time almost beyond his imagining. To the west lay Uffington Castle, an Iron Age hill-fort with its white horse carved in the chalk, and beyond that the damp, eerie tomb known as Wayland Smithy. To the east the sweep of Lowbury Hill dominated the valley. Somewhere in this wilderness of shivering grass she could be lying hurt.

In the end it was the dog he saw first, a flicker of white in the corner of his eye, away to his right. He raced diagonally up and across the slope. At first he couldn't find her but then the expected flash of red anorak pinpointed her position. She was leaning against a tree, her back to him, so that she was unaware of his approach until Robbie offered a sharp yap of welcome.

"Hello," she said flatly, as though it were a perfectly normal meeting place.

"Are you alright?"

"Yes. Why shouldn't I be?"

A wave of irrational anger burst out of him.

"What the hell are you doing up here? We've been going frantic. Your gran's in a right state and I've been looking everywhere."

"Sorry," she said. "What time is it?" He glanced down at his wrist, pushing up his sleeve to find he wasn't wearing his watch.

"It's probably at least half-past ten."

"Oh no," she cried, moving rapidly into action. "Come on, boy," she said to Robbie. She turned as if she intended to hurry back. Simon grabbed her arm roughly.

"Hey, slow down. I haven't come all the way up here just to chase you down again. What's going on?" He could have hit her. Once his dad had come looking for him, one night when he'd forgotten the time and been late. He'd said he was going to play at Mark's but, when Dad had got there, there had been no sign of him. Dad had gone to Mark's house only to find that Mark was already in bed and had not seen Simon all evening. By the time Simon turned up, having spent the evening in Karen Ballard's playroom, his parents had been desperate. They'd welcomed him home with a good hiding and sent him to bed early for a fortnight. Now he understood exactly why. "Charlie, we've been worried. Why didn't you tell your gran where you were going?"

"She was in the bathroom. I left her a note."

"Well, she didn't find it. She phoned me."

He dropped his hands to his sides. He couldn't reach her. She had become remote, separate from him. He didn't know what to say. She stood quietly at his side for a moment or two then she said softly, "Simon. I've got to go."

"OK. I'll walk back with you."

"No. I mean go away, go home."

"I know," he said, "but it's a long time till Saturday."

"Not Saturday – today, this morning! It's Dad. He's back early, on his way to pick me up."

"But he can't."

"Of course he can. The conference was boring, he flew home and rang from the airport to tell me to pack my bags. For all I know he could be there already, harassing Gran because I'm not there."

"Didn't you tell him?"

"Tell him what? Go back to Geneva because there's this boy called Simon who wants me to stay?"

"Couldn't he stay here till Saturday?"

"You have to be joking. He'll be back at work tomorrow morning, or even tonight if necessary." She touched his arm. "I wanted to, really I did. I wanted to tell him to go home and leave me here to come home on the train, but he didn't give me a chance. He delivered the instructions and put the phone down. That's why I ran out. I needed to be where he couldn't find me but it's no use. I'll have to go back now."

"Why didn't you come round to me?"

"First place they'd look!"

She began to move off down the hill, solemn, dry-eyed, and defeated. Simon felt bereft. With a snap of his nasty little fingers the man had taken away the best thing that had ever happened, leaving so much unsaid, so much undone.

"I had it all planned," he said to wide open spaces. "It isn't fair!" He felt his throat tighten and close. "Oh God! Please, not tears!" and as if on cue they sprang hotly, blurring the trees and the smooth curve of the ridge, blinding him. She moved inexorably from him in a shimmer of red and he was powerless to stop it.

He began to run, eastwards along the escarpment, accelerating, pounding the turf like a racehorse blinkered and spurred. It wasn't fair! Nothing, nothing was ever fair.

"Simon, wait!" she yelled but the words were lost in a rush of wind and the thudding in his head and all the while Robbie threaded between them like a little snowy shuttle.

He never knew what tripped him but suddenly the world slipped its axis and he was flying and then rolling, tumbling, steamrollering through long, wet grass. He lay where he stopped, winded and stunned, probably hurt, unwilling to stir, and he gave himself up to all the grief and anger of a lifetime. "Don't you believe in Fate?" she had asked him. Well, now he knew that the fate of Simon Walters was pre-ordained. It was his destiny that all who cared for him should be taken from him. He should have known better. How had he let her slip under his guard? Cocooned in a green cave, his face pressed to the musty earth, he howled at last, as if the shock of the fall had finally uncorked him.

By the time Charlie reached him he was helpless, unable to stop or to hide his humiliation. He didn't hear her, only felt her touch as she slithered down beside him. As she cradled him to her he buried his face in her shoulder, smothering the sound but unable to prevent the shuddering breaths from heaving his body. She was stroking his hair, smoothing her hand across his back, and all the time saying nothing at all. He felt rescued, like a child again. But he wasn't a child. He was aware of his cheek pressed against the soft swell of her breast. He was exactly where he wanted to be but his nose was running and he knew his eyes would be red and swollen. This pathetic vision of himself provoked a fresh flood. "I'm sorry," he burbled. "I'm sorry."

"It's alright," Charlie whispered, her mouth close to his ear. "It's alright," and she breathed softly beside him until the shaking stopped and the aching sobs died away in his throat.

He felt the need to explain, to find the words to explain it all.

"My mother's dead," he said.

"I know," she crooned, stuffing a hanky into his fist. It was a tiny, embroidered ladies' handkerchief but better than nothing. Without allowing her to see his face he tried to clean himself up. There was nothing else to say, except to make sure that she understood.

"I didn't want you to go."

"I know." She sat patiently beside him on the grass, giving him time, fondling Robbie absent-mindedly.

"Will you ever come back?"

"I promise."

"When?"

"When I can."

"Will he let you?"

"I'm nearly seventeen, Simon. I've told you I'll be back." There was so much he might have said but he didn't. He let her kiss him gently, afraid to gather her in as he felt the tears well once more. He watched her stand up and straighten her clothing and, without moving, he let her walk away. She turned to wave to him once, just before she disappeared where the slope grew steeper, and he waved back, as cheerfully as he could. In his mind's eye he was with her every step of the way but he felt too tired to chase after her, and too raw around the edges to take any more. The breeze swirled along the bank, wrenching at his hair and whipping at his skin. There was rain in the wind.

Chapter
FOURTEEN

"Hi. Happy birthday," sang a familiar far-away voice.

"Hi, big sister. Thanks."

"How has it been so far?" Suzie enquired.

"I've just got in from school. I stayed for rugby practice. Rotten sods gave me the bumps."

"Have you recovered?"

"Yes, just about. Thanks for the card." She'd signed it, in her usual neat round writing, 'Love from Suzie and Bruce'. After all those years of 'Love Suzie' she had suddenly become half of a pair. It had shocked him just as much as his father's lonely signature which had brought a lump to his throat that morning. Just as his parent had become singular Suzie had also changed her status without warning and she answered now in the plural.

"We chose it specially. We've got you a present, too, but we'll bring it down when we come in a couple of weeks."

"What is it?"

"Wait and see. Is Dad taking you out anywhere?"

"Yeah, for a meal. Kev's coming too."

"Dad said you didn't want a party. Where are you going?"

"Don't know. I think it's supposed to be a surprise."

"Had any nice presents?"

"Not yet. There wasn't much time this morning. Dad says I can have them when he gets home."

"Are you both alright?"

"Yeah, fine."

"Dad says your friend has gone back home."

"Yeah."

"But you're alright?"

"Yes, thanks. Are you?"

When she'd eventually rung off he went back to his room to finish his coffee and peruse his cards once more. Dad's and Suzie's were both humorous, chosen with care to amuse him. Grandma's was old-fashioned with a sentimental little verse to tell him he was wonderful, probably purchased from the dusty racks at the corner shop, but it had a cheque in it. Aunt Jane had remembered, too, and his Godparents. He'd probably get one from his Uncle Dick in Devon before too long. He never forgot but never got the date right either. He sent cards that said, 'I used to think Amnesia was rice pudding until I forgot your birthday' or 'I didn't forget your birthday. I only forgot the date.' The surprises were the one from Mrs. Green next door, with a five pound note in it, and the three from school – a rude one from Kev and his mum, an 'I am 6' badge converted to 16 on a card from Maureen and a third one signed by the rest of the gang with some dubious messages. He wondered if Charlie had thought about him at all. He wished he could tell her he was sixteen now. He felt older. He wished he could tell her that last Thursday wasn't her fault.

The day she had left he had watched her walk away, back to her real world, while he sat numbly on the slope like some abandoned pet. It had been quite a time, he didn't know how long, before he had stirred himself to face the journey home, which in itself had been a nightmare of anxiety in case he met someone he knew. There was no way that he could have explained his appearance and yet when he tried a brief run, to lessen the chance of any unwanted encounter, his legs didn't want to move and at least half of him was past caring anyway. Only the remnants of the pride which had aided him in the past ensured that he reached home unmolested. He'd thought of calling in at Kev's cottage for a wash but couldn't face the inevitable explanation and the thought of the sisters listening in. He'd put his head down and walked steadily, never looking up to see who was around. He even thought he'd heard his name called once but it wasn't repeated and he just kept going. With his own front door closed firmly behind him, in the sanctuary of the hall, he breathed deeply and for the first time blessed the solitude of the empty house.

He was wet through to his underwear and stiff. His limbs felt heavy. His mind seemed to have switched into a stand-by phase in which thoughts waited in limbo but couldn't yet find expression. Only the physical discomfort prompted him into rational action and he dragged himself upstairs and prepared a hot bath as she had once recommended. He stayed in it a long time and as the body thawed, the brain unlocked itself. She had held him to her, waited with him as long as she dared and accepted his outburst not with horror or embarrassment but with all the consideration he could have hoped for. He, in return, had responded to her news like a selfish child, seeing only the collapse of his own dreams, feeling only his own loss. He'd let her go back alone, picturing her route but not sharing it, not telling her that he didn't blame her. She was half-way to Chester and it was too late.

Dried and dressed at last, he had attempted to pick up the threads again. The carefully prepared tray in the kitchen he decided to leave. He'd make a pot of tea when he heard his dad's car in the drive. He took a couple of apples and a packet of crisps as his lunch and headed back upstairs, intending to read enough to allow him to start a literature essay later on but his mind refused to be guided. He found he'd read twenty pages and could remember virtually nothing of what they said. Eventually he went back to his essay about the horses on the Downs. He was appalled by its paucity of description and realised that by reliving the events of the morning he could produce something of a quite different nature. In searching for Charlie he'd looked and listened like never before. He began the essay again and this time, though the horses featured briefly, it became a search for an injured child in amongst the trees, bushes and swishing grasses of the ridge. It was a mark of his mood that the child should be found dead in the last line but even so he felt he had avoided the worst excesses of overwriting. It was the best thing he had ever done. Rereading it he was surprised by the tension he had created. If nothing else, today might have earned him a Grade A for at least one piece of work. He glanced up and caught sight of his Brueghel picture on the wall.

In idle moments over the months he'd used his vast collection of felt-tips to fill in the shapes and, although it was nowhere near completion, its pale outlines had given way to splashes of psychedelic colour. A lime-green shepherd tended a flock of multi-coloured sheep. He regretted that. It was a tasteless amendment, a pointless vandalism committed during a very boring Sunday, but he liked the glossy black ship that rode the turquoise sea, its golden sails billowing out towards the distant city that he had enhanced in shades of lemon and creamy white, like Greek villas trapped in sunlight. Against the deep greens of the foliage that he had realistically and meticulously coloured in on one of his more responsible days, the blobs of bright pink, purple and crimson looked incongruous, almost offensive, and he suddenly saw the body of his fictional child with startling clarity, an intrusive presence in a natural landscape. 'She lay, tiny and crumpled, like a sweet wrapper in the whispering grass,' he wrote and then ruled off with one decisive stroke. By the time his father came home he had conquered the morning's gloom, he thought.

They had eaten their evening meal together at the kitchen table. Simon had cooked egg and chips while his father showered and changed. Neither of them had said a great deal but that wasn't unusual. They each had their own preoccupations and it often took his dad a while to unwind and put the day behind him. Eventually Simon asked, "What time are you going out?"

"About half an hour or so. What time is Charlie coming?" His father got up to put his dishes in the sink and Simon was grateful that he had his back to him.

"She's not."

"Why not? I thought you two wanted a bit of time to yourselves."

"She's gone home. Her dad came to fetch her this morning."

"Was that on the cards? I thought she said she was staying all week."

"She was. He just changed his plans and carried her off. She doesn't seem to have much option where he's concerned."

"Well, at least you can concentrate on your schoolwork for a change."

"Why not? There's nothing else in this world likely to matter." He joined his father by the sink and nudged him out of the way to get at the washing-up. "Go on. I'll do these. I've got nothing else to do now."

"What time did she leave?"

Simon shrugged lethargically. "Just before lunch I think. Don't know exactly."

"Are you going to keep in touch with each other?"

"Don't know..." He didn't trust himself to go on. He bit his lip and shook his head. He felt his father go out of the room and shut the kitchen door behind him and he appreciated the chance to pull himself together. By the time he returned Simon had recovered his composure. He had broken the news. He wouldn't have to talk about it any more. He knew his father would treat it seriously and not make fun of him. It was something in the quiet way he had made his exit. "Who were you phoning?" Simon asked.

"Just cancelling out this evening. Thought I'd stay in for a change."

"You don't have to stay in for me, really. I'm OK, Dad," but his dad had stayed in and he'd listened quietly without interrupting while Simon recounted the day's trauma. "She was so easy to talk to, you know. You didn't have to put on an act with her." He'd suddenly found himself talking in the past tense as if she had dropped out of his world for ever and wondered if it were an omen.

"Why don't you invite her down again? If her father won't let her stay here she could stay with her gran, surely?"

"She might not want to come."

"You'll never know if you don't ask."

"She's probably furious with me. I wasn't very helpful." He hadn't gone as far as admitting to the crying. "I just felt angry and let down, didn't think about how she was feeling."

"We are all guilty of that. How will she know you're sorry unless you tell her?"

"I don't know her address."

"But you know someone who does." Simon had pondered on the pros and cons of approaching Mrs. Hadley already. "It's up to you anyway but I'd certainly make the effort if it were me."

"Well, you would!" They'd grinned at each other, fellow conspirators in the battle of the sexes. "Yeah, OK, I'll go and see her soon." They'd spent the rest of the evening chatting about life, the universe, schoolwork and everything. Simon had even let him read the essay and was pleased to see his father visibly impressed.

"There's hope for you yet," he conceded. "Tomorrow we'll go to the library and get your books and over the weekend we'll do what we can."

"Aren't you going to work?"

"No. I'm spending the day with my son. I'm sure I can feel a touch of 'flu coming on." Simon could hardly believe what he was hearing but they had really spent the next day together, trundling first around Newbury and then coming home with a take-away to an evening of sorting out his work and planning the History project.

"You're very good at this sort of thing," Simon commented. "When did you learn how to sort information like this. You make it seem straightforward."

"What do you think I spend my days doing if it is not trying to make sense out of volumes of paperwork?"

"Doesn't it drive you crazy?"

"Yes, of course it does, but we have to eat, don't we, and it pays for a crust. You can go a long way if you know how to communicate."

"That's what Mrs. Davies keeps telling us."

"Then believe the lady!"

"If you could choose again would you still do the same thing?" He'd never thought his father's life sounded particularly interesting but they'd not discussed it before. Simon had no clear idea what he wanted to do but a fairly clear idea of the kind of office job he didn't want.

"No. I don't imagine there are many people around who are completely satisfied with the way their lives have turned out, though that's not the same as being unhappy. Things could have been a lot worse but they might have been better too."

"What would you have liked to do?"

"Something where success is related to talent and effort instead of luck or other people's judgement." Simon remembered Suzie's warning about his father feeling past it. He hadn't heard him sound disillusioned before. His dad had always seemed to be tough and resilient. He'd even handled Mum's death remarkably well once the initial shock had worn off.

"What kind of job would that be?"

"If I knew I'd have gone off to do it. It's not a fair world."

"You're telling me!"

"But you give yourself a better chance with a good education. At least you have some choices if you have qualifications."

"Now you're trotting out the same old line, Dad."

"Alright – no more moaning. Go and make us both a drink."

When he came back with two mugs of hot chocolate they sat companionably in front of the fire. Simon was trying to remember when they had last had a real conversation or deliberately made time for each other. The evening meal with Charlie on Wednesday had been the first time for months and yet here they were, two days later, sharing their lives again.

"I wonder where Mum is now?" he ventured.

"Wherever we are, I should think." Simon nodded agreement. Somewhere in his head he carried that knowledge of her which could surface at any time, to guide him or chide him, and that vision, too, which had sharpened into focus in a dingy pub which she had never set foot in, because that's where he happened to be.

"She's alright, you know." His dad didn't answer but he knew he was listening. "Even when I first found her, that day, she looked really calm and peaceful, sort of blank." They both sipped their drinks and stared absently at the electric bars. A shimmer of heat rose and danced along the mantelpiece before dispersing into the air above them. He wondered if that was what people left behind them, a kind of current of energy that you could only see under certain circumstances. "Do you believe in ghosts?" he asked.

"No," said his father, with the same certainty with which he had replied to Charlie's question, "but as long as I live she'll be around. You can't wipe out her influence. Without her we would have been different people, wouldn't we?"

"You might have been. I wouldn't have existed at all."

"There you are then."

They hadn't talked much after that, each of them wallowing in their own recollections, but Simon had felt at home again, there in the armchair opposite his father, their long legs stretched out before them so that their feet almost touched in the middle of the hearthrug. Simon looked across and saw how he would be.

They'd worked as a team all weekend, Simon writing,

discussing a little, writing some more and ticking off the plan as he whittled away at the sections of his project, his father cooking, supplying coffee, checking his work and advising. Charlie was never far from his thoughts and, though he did his best to concentrate, his stomach churned each time the phone rang, but she didn't call and his resolve weakened with each passing hour. If she wanted to talk to him she would. How could he bother Mrs. Hadley for her address or phone number after the way he had treated her? He even remembered shouting at her, for worrying them unnecessarily, without bothering to find out why she'd gone in the first place. He decided to wait a few days and see what happened, then perhaps he and Kev could make a pact. They'd both got difficult letters to write. They could dare each other.

The day of his birthday had been odd though it wasn't something he could explain, not even to Suzie. He was glad of the distractions of school and for minutes at a time he had forgotten the date, Charlie's continuing silence and the cake his mother would have baked. He had agreed with his father that he'd wait until the evening for his presents. It felt like an adult's birthday. He'd often wondered what it felt like not to be excited, ever since the day he'd run in to his dad with a card and a present at eight o'clock one Sunday morning to find that his dad had genuinely forgotten what day it was. It had seemed quite unbelievable at the time.

He liked the sweatshirt that his father brought home almost as much as the cassette player, and he was pleased to find the large pack of blank tapes that Aunt Jane had thoughtfully provided. He liked the idea of the family conspiracy to make him happy. They had obviously consulted each other. Grandma's cheque could go towards tapes, too. When Kevin arrived just after seven he handed Simon a small, squashy parcel. It turned out to be a T-shirt with a slogan – 'It's hard to be humble when you are as great as I am!'

"Thanks, Kev. What a tasteful little number!" He

wanted to put it on but his dad insisted on something smart, especially as Kevin had resorted to a jacket and tie, though it was a bow tie and bright red. Simon lingered in his room while Kevin and his father waited below. He reached out the suit he had worn only once before, put it back and then took it out again. He dressed quickly before he could change his mind and hurried down, praying that his dad wouldn't comment. He saw the appreciative glance but nothing was said.

"Are we ready then?" Mike Walters patted his pocket, checking for car keys. Simon was reaching for the doorknob just as the bell rang.

It was Mrs. Hadley, huddled in a very familiar red jacket, and looking very small in the doorway. The proportions of the cottage suited her better, Simon thought. She pulled back anxiously on the lead as Robbie tried to clamber up the step.

"Hello," Simon said. "We were just going out. Come in." He realised immediately what he'd said and flushed guiltily as she politely refused.

"No, I won't stay if you don't mind. Robbie and I enjoy our evening walk. I'm glad I just caught you, though. Charlotte said I was to be sure to get it to you today and I was so worried when it hadn't arrived by lunch-time. The second post comes any time these days, I'm afraid, and sometimes not at all, but when I got back from the shops there it was on the step." She held out a squarish package done up in brown paper and yards of sticky tape. It was addressed to him care of the cottage.

"Thanks," he said.

"She said she'd sent it to me as she wasn't certain of your exact address and didn't want it to go astray. At least I can report it has been safely delivered." She smiled kindly. "May I wish you a happy birthday too, Simon dear," and she took a small card from her jacket pocket and handed it to him shyly. "Good night," she said. "Have a good evening all of you," and she turned briskly.

"Good night," Simon called.

"Well, well!" said his father. Kevin looked bemused.

"It's a long story, mate," Simon explained as Mike closed the front door gently.

"Come on then. Open it."

It took time to wrench the sticky tape free and get at the contents and even then he found more wrapping paper and a card. He opened the card first, aware of two pairs of eyes watching his fumbling fingers, and he tried hard to keep the smile off his face. He read it and then handed it to his father. It said, 'Roll on Christmas, lots of love, C. XXX' and the picture on the front had been specially concocted. A Golden Retriever peered soulfully out at him and by its side Charlie had pasted a picture of a bright-eyed West Highland Terrier that she must have cut from another card.

"Why's she done this?" his father asked, running his fingers across the glued-on dog, but Simon didn't answer immediately. He was unfolding a dark-blue woollen scarf. It was soft and expensive and as he draped it across his arm two bits of paper fluttered to the floor. Kevin bent to pick one up and Simon retrieved the other. He read, "'This is to replace your scarf which I intend to keep,'" and Kevin handed him a couple of folded sheets covered with minute printing. They were railway timetables and she had high-lighted some of the columns, detailing the journey from Reading to Chester via several trains.

"What's going on?" Kevin enquired. "Am I allowed to know?"

Simon stood his two new cards on the hall table, pushed the papers into his silky new pocket, hung the scarf around his neck and reached out. As they moved towards the door he grasped them both firmly, an arm round each of his friends.

"C'mon, team," he said. "Let's go!"

DOWNSTREAM
John Rowe Townsend

Alan Dollis is seventeen and bored. His family's recent move to a quiet riverside village has left him between schools and between friends. But two unexpected events bring the summer alight. First, his father buys an old boat-house and then his German tutor, Mrs Briggs, turns out to be a sensational and explosive surprise…

"A powerful, passionate and masculine novel … Townsend's craftsmanship and empathy with his hero make *Downstream* outstanding."
The Sunday Times

THE FIRST TIME
Aisling Foster

It's the summer term at William Stubbs Comprehensive and romance is in the air. Not for Rosa, though – style and painting are the loves of her life. But, as Rosa's sex maniac mum keeps telling her, there's a first time for everything. The important thing is to get it right...

"Brilliant and affectionate style-wars novel."
The Sunday Telegraph

MORE WALKER PAPERBACKS

For You to Enjoy